NEWTON'S SWING

Chris Paling is the author of *After the Raid, Deserters, Morning All Day* and *The Silent Sentry.*

ALSO BY CHRIS PALING

Chris Paling

NEWTON'S SWING

V

VINTAGE

Published by Vintage 2001

2 4 6 8 10 9 7 5 3 1

Copyright © Chris Paling 2000

Grateful acknowledgement is made to the following for permission to reprint previously published material:

Lyrics from 'Aja' (Becker/Fagen) © 1977 by kind permission of Universal/MCA Music Ltd

Excerpt from *The Anatomy Lesson*, © 1983 by Philip Roth, reprinted by permission of Random House

First published in Great Britain by
Jonathan Cape 2000

Vintage
Random House, 20 Vauxhall Bridge Road,
London SW1V 2SA

Random House Australia (Pty) Limited
20 Alfred Street, Milsons Point, Sydney
New South Wales 2061, Australia

Random House New Zealand Limited
18 Poland Road, Glenfield, Auckland 10, New Zealand

Random House (Pty) Limited
Endulini, 5A Jubilee Road, Parktown 2193, South Africa

The Random House Group Limited Reg. No. 954009
www.randomhouse.co.uk

A CIP catalogue record for this book
is available from the British Library

ISBN 0 09 928444 8

The Random House Group Limited supports The Forest Stewardship Council (FSC®), the leading international forest certification organisation. Our books carrying the FSC label are printed on FSC® certified paper. FSC is the only forest certification scheme endorsed by the leading environmental organisations, including Greenpeace. Our paper procurement policy can be found at www.randomhouse.co.uk/environment

MIX
Paper from
responsible sources
FSC® C018072
www.fsc.org

Printed and bound in Great Britain by Clays Ltd, St Ives PLC

For Julie

... and finally, having lost what was to be lost, my torn and black heart rebels, saying enough already, enough, this is as low as I go.

George Saunders
The Wavemaker Falters

1. Newton's Swing

BROWN MOTHS PINCH the air around the Keegans' front door. They fly like folding leaves in the soft glow of the porch light. To the east, the Atlantic rolls back and forth over the New England shore, furling and unfurling its welcome mat. It was the ocean that claimed the life of Newton B. Keegan, only son of Maude and Henry. He was six years old. His death claimed their lives too and both of them are facing this truth in different ways. Maude is thirty-one, Henry is two years her senior but appears twenty years older. They own a store in a row of other small one-storey stores (a chandler's, a deli, a bookshop and an antiques mart that opens only in the season and seems to trade only to those people who are down for the season). Henry and Maude sell groceries and postage stamps, fishing nets, bright blue buckets and shrimp nets. Their stock of beach balls and lilos is tied to the post beside the door. When the breeze gets up along the coast the lilos dance and the balls keep time. Children stand and watch. The salt has stripped the store of its paint but Henry doesn't prime and fill the wood any more, he blows off the topcoat of varnish with a heat-gun and paints another on. The front of the store looks as rugged and weathered as an old yacht. Over the window is a sign,

'Keegan's General Store, est. 1991'. Henry Keegan used to make people smile with his cautious witticisms. He's a large man with a thick black beard, he wears a dark suede waistcoat over his paunch. People used to say he looked like a saloon keeper or a tough frontiersman. His laugh could be as loud as the tenor foghorn that calls from down the coast when the mist comes in, as it did on the day that Newton died.

I can see Henry across the street. He's staring at the coals in his barbecue. They are glowing orange because Henry has just blown the white dust from them. Some of the dust has silted his eyes and he rubs his sleeve across his face but his eyes continue to sting and Henry knows he has been crying again. Sometimes he can't stop. He goes alone to cry in the cold, windowless room at the back of the store. When you ring the brass bell on the counter, if Henry doesn't come out straight away to serve you, you wait until he does. He looks right at you these times, challenging you not to offer the sympathy you feel for this huge, broken man. His blue eyes are dull. They lie sunk in the black of his eye sockets like jewels in a corroded bracelet brought up from a wreck.

Henry used to make me feel small. Not just physically, he also made my life seem small. I used to feel that nothing big enough would ever come along to knock Henry off his feet. I hurt easily. So does my son, Jordan. He's a bright wiry kid, all arms and legs, elbows and knees. He can run faster than the other kids. Sometimes he used to run just for the hell of it. And he laughed a lot too. Less so now, of course. Jordan, who's eleven years old, used to hang out with Newton even though the Keegans' son was a few years younger.

Sometimes Henry and Maude would argue, but it was only Maude's voice you could hear across the street; loud and shrill, and you could sense Henry calming her. 'You make me scream,' she shouted one night, 'because you're so *even*. Why do I have to do the screaming for both of us?'

Now she doesn't scream at all. She sleepwalks through the town, back and forth along the middle of the hot street to the library; two, three times a week. The locals look out for her when they drive into town. She just smiles when strangers honk their horn at her ('Hey lady, trying to get yourself killed?'), but the smile is fixed like it's been painted on. The drugs do that.

Maude used to help out in the white clapboard library, now she stays home reading her borrowed books. This week she's carrying a stack of French literature. Her friend, senior librarian Charlotte Cale, has made out a reading list for her. Henry says it seems she can no longer make any decisions for herself. So Charlotte – indomitable Charlotte with her Boston ways and selective snobbery – is mapping a route for Maude back to rude health (her concept) through the byways of European Literature. She's already worked through the brooding Russians, now she's taking on the slippery Frenchies. Soon she'll be well enough to find her way through Faulkner again and tackle the gentle brutality of Hemingway. Charlotte maybe will ease her in with some barbed Scott Fitzgerald. One day, when she can make the choices for herself, Charlotte will be glad to see her select a little Anne Tyler from the carousel of bright paperbacks by the check-out desk.

Two years ago today, Newton died.

'Hey, Henry. How's it going?' I call and wander over the narrow street, watching for fast cars cutting back from the high street trying to jump the queue for the last ferry. The sky is an ocean of black. If you look hard at it you can see the clouds skimming the surface. Henry stares at me for a while as though he can't put a name to the face then nods a gentle, 'OK, John.' He pushes at the coals with his tongs, picks one up, examines it close to his eyes and lays it back down again like it's a piece of meat cooking in the heart of the fire. 'Help

3

yourself to a beer,' Henry says, and points to a bucket by the white table. It's half-full of iced water, a stash of brown bottles at the bottom like lobsters in a restaurant tank.

'Can I get one for you?' I ask him.

'Sure, why not?'

I'm not familiar with the brand. I open two bottles with the army knife on Henry's big ring of keys. The round white table is set for one. Rust bleeds through the rim. Beside the table is one chair. Two more stand in the middle of the brown dry lawn, shadowed by the trees. They are angled towards each other: a stage set for a tough conversation or a session with a psychiatrist. Behind them, Newton's swing hangs still.

I know that Henry has eaten alone. He wanted to mark the night somehow, but Maude was asleep as usual and Henry couldn't face letting it go by so he went to the trouble of lighting his old barbecue (an oil-drum cut in half), waiting for the coals to burn white and cooking his slab of steak. He wanted to do it right so he made a green salad to go with it. Some of the leaves are left in the glass bowl on the table. Beside the salad, a bottle of dressing. The cork is dark with congealed oil. Henry's white plate is juiced with red from his rare steak.

I hand Henry a beer, he holds it in his thick fingers and tears of iced water spill down his knuckles. He stares at it, drinks down a long draught, holds back a belch.

'Don't mind me,' I say. At times like this I'm reminded that I'm an Englishman. Usually I forget. Henry roars a belch into the night. A dog barks in the wire compound behind the fish restaurant.

We hear the horn from the ferry; the line of cars starting their engines; the chains and metallic crash as the ferry drops its drawbridge onto the concrete quay. A radio ignites with the call-sign of a local station, then a DJ crooning a message

4

of love as he introduces the Supremes: 'This one goes out to you, Blue, from you know who.' He's been listening to too many other DJs playing the same tunes. Now he doesn't know who he is, hearing his own voice through the headphones, night after night after night.

'Baby love,' Henry says and tries to laugh. He sounds like a smoker who has smoked too much. Then he strolls over to the seats on the lawn and pulls one square on to the house, but he doesn't sit down. Instead, he comes walking back towards me saying, 'I asked her to stay up with me.' I nod. 'But she says she has to sleep through it. You see that's the way she deals . . .' He stops, shakes his head, and looks down at the lawn. '. . . But it's not dealing with it, John. I want my boy back. And I want Maude back. And I know I have to come to terms with what happened to Newton, but I need Maude to help me to do that.' He looks back towards the house, hoping by some miracle she's heard him. The blinds stay shut.

'Why don't you let me buy you a beer?' I offer, not expecting Henry to take it up. He looks back at the dark house once more then heads off towards the main street. I call to him that I'll catch him up after I ask old Mrs Lomax to keep an eye on Jordan. She's in her small kitchen greasing a tin and singing along tremulously and insanely high to the country music on the radio. I tell her I'm taking Henry for a beer and before I have to ask the favour she says she'll gladly mind the boy. The light is on in his room. He's reading or watching the portable TV or, knowing Jordan, maybe both. I promised him I'd go in and say goodnight and I feel guilty about that but there is no time because Henry is already out of sight, striding towards the heart of the small town.

I catch him at the corner where he's stopped to watch the last of the cars turn onto the quay road. The ferry sounds its horn again, then the engines roar as it backs out into the black tide. The diesels spit up a sudden slick of white foam. The ferry turns and heads away. When it has gone the town is quiet again, just the measured voices coming from the veranda of the fish restaurant and the good-natured clamour from the bar next door. Henry heads for the bar, a white colonial building with a draped Stars and Stripes hanging from a long horizontal staff. When he gets to the door he stops and looks back along the street, then he goes in.

We don't know what happened to Newton. Nobody knows except Henry because Henry was out there alone with his son in his boat. The sea was not angry on the day Newton was lost but there was a mist. Henry and Newton sometimes headed up the estuary to catch crayfish, but on that day they went out to sea. Henry was soaked through when he came back late that night. He went to call the police, the police called the coastguard. Through the night you could hear the helicopters sweeping up and down the coast, playing searchlights over the waves. I couldn't sleep so I watched from my window. At daybreak the coastguard drove up in his land-cruiser and went to Henry's door. I saw him compose himself, run his finger round his shirt collar, pat down the sweat wedge of his hair before knocking. Henry answered. The man said something. Henry stood aside to let him in. The door closed.

By midday the town knew that the body of Newton Keegan had been found washed up on the shore three miles north of the town. The news reports said that the boy was fully clothed. I don't suppose they meant anything by it but the mention of the boy's clothing got people talking and opened up all kinds of speculation that Henry and Maude could have done without. It didn't last, except in the minds of people who need to believe the worst of others just to make their own lives more bearable.

★

6

When Henry walks into the bar nobody stops talking. The piano does not stop playing. It is no big deal for anybody except for Henry. This is because the bar is full of visitors; holidaymakers in their tan deck shoes and chinos, striped French sweaters knotted round their waists; an older couple in shorts, looking round like they don't belong but want to. A man with a sunburnt bald head punches his friend on the shoulder. Henry buys the drinks and I sit beside him on a tall stool at the bar. I can smell the beer-wet wood of the bar floor.

Henry drinks his beer. We don't talk. It feels like he's using muscles he hasn't used for a while, just being there among strangers. I buy another beer. Then Henry asks me about the agency, about Susan's death and I fill him in. I don't tell him about Carol because I tell nobody about Carol. That way it stays safe and even though Carol rarely ventures outside of New York City, rumours don't respect city boundaries. I don't want to jeopardise Carol's marriage and, unsurprisingly, she doesn't want it either. Henry gives the matter some thought. He says I should bring Jordan round to see Maude. He asks before he has a chance to check himself, some of the old Henry coming through. And I say I will, I'll bring him around before we go back to the city, and we leave it there. Henry doesn't talk about the night Newton died, but something loosens in him as we sit at the bar buying beers. He drinks five or six bottles. I lose count.

On the way home I get to thinking about Newton, how he must have gone over the side, dropped down like he was weighted with an anvil round his ankles. I see his small head disappearing fast into the black and Henry, frantic, jumping over after him: diving, diving. Coming up for air, but too much darkness beneath him to find his son. I conjecture that, exhausted, he would have sat in the boat for a while wondering how he was going to break it to Maude before turning on the engine and heading home. Maybe in the time I spent with Henry the story just transferred itself between us, in the space between the words we were using; in the half-smiles, the one time he laughed gently.

When we get back to the house Jordan's light is out. I say goodnight to Henry and shake his hand. He looks over at Newton's swing. I think he half-hopes Maude will be there, waiting for him to come home: better; healed. Or maybe he hopes for something more. That one day the swing will ride high again, carrying Newton up towards the stars, then back down again so Henry can lift him gently to the ground and hold him tight to his heart one last time.

2. Susan's Death – Version 1

SOME MINUTES HAVE passed since I have dialled 911. I sit in the bedroom looking at Susan lying on the bed. I don't know what else I can do. Jordan is asleep in his room next door and I don't want to wake him. At the same time I don't want him to walk in on the paramedics massaging her heart or whatever it is they'll have to do. So I sit, stand, turn off the light, go to the window. Over the street somebody is holding a party. It looks like silhouettes of people have been cut out and pasted on the tall apartment windows. Piano music floats this way. Occasionally the summer breeze tugs some of the frequencies away towards the East River.

My shirt is wet with fear. I can smell my fear; taste it. I go to the bed, pull the sheets up to Susan's chin the way I do when she's ill and she wants me to look after her. I can't feel the sadness yet. I can't feel anything. Yes I can but I don't want to acknowledge it. I hear the piano again and it makes me wonder what kind of people own the party apartment. Nobody hires a pianist nowadays. I waste emotion on it. These things matter. In my profession your antenna is tuned to the nuances of change.

I hear the door buzzer. I run down the stairs and pull open the door. A short woman stands there; stocky, brutal haircut, piggy eyes. An ambulance boy is behind her with a bag. His Jimmy Olsen face shines with excitement. I wait for them to tell me what to do. I feel my heart through my chest, I smell the sweat on me. I point up the stairs. She pushes past and I read something in the look she gives me. Maybe she is trained to be suspicious, maybe it's just paranoia. I step out into the street and look at my watch. It's 3.17 a.m. So why am I dressed?

Why *am* I dressed?

I breathe in the night air and taste the cold metal of old traffic fumes. A street lunatic soft-shoe shuffles by. A couple come out of the party block. He's drunk, she is not. He has his arm round her neck. He's a big man carrying too much weight. He's wearing a tuxedo and a yellow waistcoat. His red bow-tie is loose. I don't know how she is supporting his weight. A cab comes up, she helps him in. The cab goes off, she stands watching it. I go over to her. I want to do it to her – there and then. To drill her against the wall. Pull up her skirt, rip off her underwear and just do it. She holds her hand out, I touch my palm against hers.

Is this how it happened?

This is how I meet Carol. On the day Susan dies. Before she is even cold, before Jordan has been told. Before the court case, before the questions. Before all of that I am standing palm-to-palm with a woman I have only just met. Then the ambulance boy comes out of my apartment (already mine, no longer ours) and says I should come in. I say to Carol, 'I'm sorry, I have to go. My wife is dead.' And Carol laughs because she imagines I am joking. I shrug and smile and go in. She never forgives herself for this lapse of taste.

When we make love for the first time we hold our hands palm-to-palm.

3. Agency – Breakfast

AT THE AGENCY, breakfast is ritual. Angel likes us to get together at around 8.15. Michael arrives first. He drives in to the city, a forty-three-mile journey that costs him anything up to two and a half hours. The price he pays for a life in the leafy suburbs is around twenty hours a week. He leaves his three daughters and his wife, Rosa, waking. Eager to hold on to his job he makes sure Angel finds him working when he arrives. Michael is the only one of us who habitually wears a necktie. He also wears black braces, an affectation that endears him to Angel who wears them himself. Michael is thirty-six years old. Whatever he does, he does fast. Michael's ideas flow quickly. Somebody pinned up a cartoon of him when we were working on our last car campaign. He was standing in a wind tunnel, his sharp nose cutting through the air and throwing a slipstream behind him.

Michael's biggest anxieties are firstly losing his job and secondly losing what remains of his fine fair hair. I tell him he need not worry. On the first account, Angel loves him like a son. On the second, he has the kind of facial bone structure that does not need hair to make it appealing. If he shaved off all of his hair you wouldn't notice.

'What do you think?' he asks.

'Shave it.'

'Should I do it?'

'Try it.'

He thinks about it for two days (a period punctuated by a number of extra visits to the washroom). On the third morning he announces to the breakfast meeting that Rosa and the girls talked about it over dinner and they made the decision that he should try it (in my head I see the meal and I do not like what I see). Angel, who is sitting at the head of the table with Michael to his right, reaches over and clasps his shoulder. From Michael's reaction, it seems he finds the gesture fatherly. I, and I suspect the others round the table, choose to see it as Angel asking Michael to keep his domestic life out of the breakfast meeting. Michael, therefore misreading the situation badly, relates further details of the meal — meatloaf — and offers a selection of the arguments pro and anti. He concludes that Rosa made the final judgement. Angel announces with finality that he could have predicted this outcome and closes the conversation by pulling out his glasses and reading out loud a piece from the *New York Times* on the new man at J. Walter Thompson.

Rosa, incidentally, respects my sartorial taste. She reached this judgement following a conversation we had one Christmas in Mort's, an Upper East Side restaurant. Michael had been asking Susan and me to go out with him and Rosa for six months. At first I passed it off as politeness. Home and work do not mix and I assumed that Michael understood this. Rosa, however, did not, which is why her entreaties to him and his to me became more persistent. I mentioned it to Susan late one night. Like Rosa, she was keen to get a glimpse into the enemy camp, so in December we met.

It was snowing and had been long enough for the novelty to wear off. The snow shovelled on the sidewalks was tainted grey with what the weather men have taken to calling particulates. It was also laser-cut with yellow dog piss. Michael had already suggested to Angel an ad in which a dog lifts its leg against a drift. When it walks away a sport logo has been scorched into the snow. Angel laughed. It was Angel's no laugh – more delighted than Angel's yes laugh, but no more real. Angel's laughter can terrify the uninitiated.

By the end of the meal, not as dull as I had feared, Rosa was drunk. She was sitting across the small table. Susan was on my right, facing Michael. I felt the side of a shoeless foot on my calf. It moved gently up and down. Rosa was smiling at me. Michael and Susan were talking about some artist or sculptor they'd discovered they both had a passion for. His name emerged as Carl Andre and Susan was asking Michael whether he saw the show at the Julian Pretto Gallery in '92. Apparently he did, he also saw the 1985 Paris show during their honeymoon. By coincidence we saw it too but I don't remember much about it. Yes I do. I remember he was the one who claims (or claimed, maybe he has other ideas now) that the ideal piece of sculpture is a road. Susan told me, as she was chewing the corner of her catalogue, that Andre worked as a freight-train brakeman. I asked her why he didn't find a job laying tarmac. That way we wouldn't be wasting an afternoon looking at this shit.

'Gallerie . . . Daniel Templon,' Susan said in her immaculate accent.

'Hey, that is right!' Michael was flushed. He used to love it when he made connections with people.

Rosa leaned towards me, I felt her right hand on my knee. Her palm was hot. 'Michael talks about you all the time,' she breathed, barely audibly. I leaned politely in. By now her hand was tightening up on my knee. I think at this point the violinist started up. The waitress was clearing the plates and smiling too hard. I sensed a sick child at home, under-provided for. She backed through the doors into the kitchen, a plate on each palm and one balanced on her arm. The smile dropped away a second before the doors swung shut.

'Robert Barry, Sylvia Mangold . . .' I heard from Susan. 'Chuck Close . . .' from Michael.

'And what does Michael say?' Having weighed up the options – pitch it loud enough to force a jovial response from Michael, thus breaking up their artsy conversation, or low enough to keep it intimate – I opted for the latter. Intimate is always best with friends' wives. They can never get enough of it and few can differentiate feigned interest from genuine. Interest, feigned or otherwise, is always seductive. It's one of the few things that make life worth living. Sex, usually, love, sometimes, interest, always.

'I sense he's a little awed by you,' Rosa said, her eyelashes flicking.

'Michael is not in awe of me. Michael is in awe of Angel. And anybody close to Angel gets some of the reflected awe.'

Rosa used to work in the city which is where she and Michael met. You can date the year they moved out by Rosa's fashion sense. She still wears the late eighties power suits when she socialises and when she comes in to the city with Michael and the girls to shop she spends increasingly long periods of time looking to buy more of these clothes. They remain available in the more expensive and conservative midtown stores to cater precisely for women like Rosa. Women who were part of it until they had children. Women who aren't part of it now.

'Abstract expressionism,' Michael said.

'Brancusi,' Susan said back.

'Susan is very beautiful,' Rosa tried, and for some reason I began to pity her girls. Perhaps I should have pitied her, I don't know.

'Yes, she is,' I said. I never owned her so I didn't feel I should take the credit. I didn't even choose her dress though she chose my suit: a four-button single-breasted charcoal grey in a material that felt like it was melting all over me like chocolate. A thousand-dollar Comme des Garçons suit.

Rosa tried another way in. 'You two seem very happy together.'

'Do we?'

'Are you?'

'People who make that statement usually aren't.'

'But what about you?'

'This evening we're happy. Yesterday we weren't. The day before that we had a few good moments but we argued in between.'

She thought about this for a moment, then said, 'So when you wake up and see Susan lying beside you, what's the first thing you think?'

'Tell me what it is you want.' I was going to go on but the thought pulled itself up short.

'From you?'

'OK.'

She laughed and leaned in, really close. 'I want you to take me to a hotel and bang my brains out.' Her hand was still on my knee. I was fairly sure Susan was unaware of this but I sensed her attention begin to home in.

'Me in particular – or anybody?' I asked her.

'What do you mean?'

'I'm saying: do you just want to be screwed or do you want to be screwed by me?'

As she contemplated this her face drained of all its colour. She said, 'I'm sorry. Excuse me,' and stood suddenly, bending and pushing the table away from her, trying to get out of the booth. She was holding a napkin to her mouth. Michael stood too. Concern, then pity, then disdain, showed on his face in descending order of sympathy. He followed her across Mort's floor. I watched them in the gilt-framed mirrors weave between the tables. The violinist stepped aside just as Rosa arched and puked her filet mignon onto the crimson carpet a few feet short of the door. Mort came from nowhere clicking his fingers over his head like castanets. The impoverished waitress arrived with a cloth. Somehow Mort's smile conveyed utter contempt towards Rosa and profound apology to the rest of his clientele. I was reading this in, I know, but it was something he did with his mouth. Susan once observed that Mort's mouth has a tough job doing the PR work for his eyes.

Michael helped Rosa through the door and out into the street. It was below zero but I knew they weren't coming back in. The violinist swung his instrument under his chin and picked it up with 'Misty' in a lilting gypsy style.

'Shit,' Susan said, and laughed into the palm of her hand. Her eyes, bright and blue, were filmed with tears of wicked mirth. We decided to sit it out for a few minutes so those who didn't already know, didn't associate us with the woman who puked on the floor. Together, unexpectedly alone, we were silent for a while. I was embarrassed by this so I asked, 'What did you make of Michael?'

'Michael?' Susan gave the question too much consideration. 'He's living with a fool which makes him unhappy. He's fighting this unhappiness at the moment for the kids, but one day he'll give in.'

'Then what?'

'I don't know Rosa. It depends how she feels about him. OK, she'll be hurt, but deep down I suspect she'll be relieved.'

Sometimes Susan used to test me like this. She'd make observations she knew I'd take personally. Usually I'd let them pass. This time I was annoyed so I said, 'You make men feel they have a chance with you. That's why they show you their unhappiness.'

'Everybody is unhappy.'

'Of course. But not all the time.'

'I didn't say they were unhappy all the time, I just said they were unhappy.'

'You implied it.'

'I didn't mean to.'

'Fine. Sorry I took it that way.'

'I have to use the bathroom.' Susan crossed the floor. Several pairs of eyes followed her. She habitually excited as much interest from women as men. Susan's beauty was what the magazines call 'natural' which made it less threatening to women and more appealing to men. Women wanted to be her friend, men wanted to drive her out to the country and roll around in a haystack with her.

I waved for the check. Mort brought it over personally. His cummerbund was ruffled. He said, 'Please tell your friend I do not want to see him on my premises again.'

'What about his wife?'

Mort was not in the mood for this. Without his customary bow, he laid the padded leather envelope on the table and walked off, picking up an empty plate from the next table and handing it to the first waiter he came to. I flicked open the envelope and winced at the bill. Susan saw the wince as she slid back into the booth. We were not poor but, like most people we knew, claimed poverty because both of us were always overdrawn on our accounts. At least Susan told me she was overdrawn when she handed over her half-share of the rent. Needless to say our finances were not conducted jointly. My suggestion, shortly after our marriage, that we open an account together was greeted with derision and my darling wife asking me whether I'd slept through the sexual revolution.

When we got outside with Michael and Rosa's coats they were gone. Susan and I debated the protocol of how we should return them. She accepted that I couldn't just bundle them into a bag and take them into work. This would have been tantamount to taking in a bucket of puke and dumping it on Michael's desk. It was, however, very cold and the weather men were predicting the temperatures would fall further. We knew Michael and Rosa would be taking the train back home so we called a cab for Grand Central Station. When we got there, Susan waited in the cab while I went in. I expected to have to search the commuter platforms but I found them on the concourse under the huge faux-winter sky. Rosa was sitting on a bench near the clock, weeping, and Michael was pacing five or six steps, back and forth, back and forth. He was angry. Rosa was so humiliated she couldn't even raise her face to look at him. I walked up to Rosa and laid Michael's coat on the bench beside her. Then I shook hers out, unpeeled the collars and stretched out the shoulders. All she had to do was stand up and inhabit it. She did, but she couldn't hold herself straight. I wanted to pat her upper arms, hold my palm to her face, do some of the things lovers do. Instead, I kissed her on the cheek, trying not to breathe in the smell of vomit. Then I turned my benevolence on Michael. I didn't want to belittle him by helping him on with his cashmere so I tossed it over for him to catch.

'Look . . .' He reached into his jacket for his wallet.

'Absolutely not, buddy.' I smiled, waved the offer away, liking myself less for the buddy.

'You must pay,' Rosa said to him.

'I insist,' Michael said.

'No. Absolutely . . .'

'Yes,' Rosa said.

'OK. If that's what you really want.' This to Michael.

'It is,' Rosa said, bitterly.

Michael held out three fifty-dollar bills. He fanned them

like a magician. I took them all and made a play of reaching in for my wallet. 'You need some change.'

'Keep it.'

'Are you sure?'

'We're sure,' Rosa said.

'OK.'

'Tell Susan . . .' Rosa looked at Michael. 'Tell her I'm sorry.'

'There's really no need.'

'Oh, but there is,' Michael insisted and I wondered how Susan had suddenly become the injured party.

'I'll tell her.'

'I should also like to call her. And . . .' Rosa said, again looking at her husband, '. . . explain.'

'John will explain,' Michael said.

'No. John will apologise. I must explain.'

I said, 'Explain it to me if you like.'

'There is nothing to explain to you. You already know.'

'Then I'll get Susan to call you. That way . . .'

'No, I'll call her,' Rosa said. 'Tomorrow.'

'OK.' I held up my hands. 'I'll tell her. Look, you two have a good journey.'

'Yes.' Michael shook my hand.

Rosa was looking up at the painted stars. She asked, 'Who would wish to paint stars on a station ceiling?'

'Some painter who needed the work,' Michael said.

Rosa panned down. 'Nice suit,' she said. And this is where her judgement of my sartorial taste was made. Under the canopy of two-and-a-half-thousand painted stars.

4. Leona

THE JURY IS still out on SoHo. This is how most
conversations regarding the district's merits usually
conclude. SoHo dinner parties habitually begin and end with
one of the guests either denigrating The Village or positing a
move to TriBeCa or the East Village. Susan was living in
SoHo when we met. We moved to a bigger apartment
shortly before Jordan's birth but neither of us wanted to leave
the area altogether. Susan worked at a number of the Greene
Street galleries and one day intended to own one herself. She
would have done, I know, had her demise not halted her
career trajectory. Susan and I, in fact, met in a gallery, Pace,
at the opening of a Claes Oldenberg show. She claimed we
had met once before but I don't remember the first meeting
even though, when she mentioned it, I said I did. She'd
dropped into the agency to talk to Angel and he introduced
us. Angel had some memory of this when I asked him. He
said he never forgets a woman's face, so I showed him a
photo of Susan and he immediately identified her.

'Yes. I know this woman. Leona.'

'Susan,' I said, taking the photograph back.

He took it back again. 'She has a mark; a birthmark, here,'
and touched his ribs, about halfway down on the left. He

walked off intoning her name. 'Leona, Leona.' Shooting a smile at the girl on the desk, he winked, touched the red rose in his lapel and turned into his office. The thick mahogany door closed with a muted clunk.

When I first arrived at the agency Angel demonstrated his door to me. 'Listen and watch,' he said. I stood at his elbow. He told the girl on the desk to hang up the phone, then he closed the door with a *clunk*, or perhaps it was more of a *chunk*. 'This is quality. Like a Mercedes,' he said. He opened the door and showed me the brass fittings and rebate of the lock. The girl at the desk chewed her thumbnail. A piece snagged between her top two teeth which she tried to flick out with her other thumbnail. When I went past her at lunch she was still trying to fillet the segment out. Later in the day I heard her talking to her boyfriend on the phone. She told him she'd got her period and that she wanted him to know so he could stop worrying. Hence the thumbnail, I expect, but not the regret in her voice. I liked that girl. She always had a smile on her face when someone came up to her desk. She said it was because she was the youngest child of three and that her parents and her brothers surrounded her with so much love when she was growing up that she came to expect the best in everybody she met. She anticipated their goodness which, in turn, tended to provoke it. I have found the converse of this also applies. The girl, whose name I forget, left a month or so after I joined. I chipped in for a present. I think I gave too much − twenty dollars − to her collection, but I wanted to celebrate her. I suppose this is another example of people who have been loved harvesting love all their lives. The unloved reap the blank looks and disapproval. When Susan and I talked about Jordan before he was born we said we would love him in part so that he would love in return. And if he loved, then he would surely be loved.

I phoned Susan. She was working at A.I.R. When she'd been called to the phone, I said, 'First, I have an apology to make.'

'Is this John?'

'That's right.'

'I'm sorry, Angela didn't get your name. She said you were some English guy.'

'Right.'

'Are we meeting again, only I had this . . .' She stopped.

'Yes?'

'It's OK, she's gone. I had this feeling that you disapproved. That's all.'

'Of you?'

'Yes. But Angela said that's just . . . look, she just came in again.'

'Shall I call back when it's more . . .?'

'No. You talk. You said something about an apology?'

'Yes. I took a photograph.'

A pause.

'Susan?'

'You took a photograph from my apartment?'

'Last night. That's why I . . .'

'From where exactly in my apartment?'

'I took it from a table. From the table by the . . .'

'You stole a fucking photograph from me?'

'I'm sorry.'

'OK, let me just, I think you should know that if you had taken the photograph from a closed drawer or a cupboard then I would have . . . Can we talk about this? I think I need to talk about this face-to-face.'

'When?'

'Which photograph did you steal?'

'Look. I didn't steal it. I borrowed it.'

'In my book, removing something from the premises of

some person or persons you do not know particularly well is stealing. Unless, of course, permission has previously been both sought and granted.'

'Susan, I'm really sorry, I just . . .'

'Is this why you called? To tell me you violated my property?'

I heard a laugh. 'Is somebody there with you?'

The receiver was covered then uncovered. 'Just Angela.'

'Does Angela know about your birthmark?'

'My . . .?'

I should perhaps have said that at this point in our relationship I had not seen Susan naked.

'Below your left breast – three, four inches down.'

'No. It's on my right side. Angela, will you please . . .' The receiver was covered again, then Susan came back, 'Are you the pervert with the telescope?'

'No. I don't have a telescope.'

'. . . Are you sure?'

'Quite sure.'

'. . . I'm sorry, I'm a little . . . OK, you know about my birthmark. So I am trying to get my head around the fact that you have been discussing my body with . . .'

'No, it just came out. In conversation. With Angel.'

'Oh, Angel.' She sounded relieved.

'Yes.'

'OK.'

When Angel met Susan the next time, two or three months into our relationship, there was a long moment between them. He called her Leona. She didn't correct him.

5. Michael's Hair

M Y GRANDFATHER WAS an engine driver. He lived with my grandmother and, for the early years of his married life, also with her mother in a small terraced house in Preston. When I was a child I often stayed with them. As a treat, my grandfather would take me with him when he went to work. I am reminded of my grandfather when I stand below the huge barrel-vaulted ceiling of Grand Central Station. When I remember my grandfather it is always winter, always early morning; dark, the black sky specked with stars. I tried to explain to Jordan what it felt like to live in the world when the night sky was dark enough to see the stars. It meant nothing to him until, one summer, we drove down to Mexico on vacation. He slept more soundly on that vacation than he has ever done since.

My grandmother would wake me at around 5 a.m. She would bring in a jug of warm water, put it on the floor and help me tug off my warm pyjamas. I would wash. She would dry me and then, fully dressed, I would go down the narrow stairs to find my grandfather at the kitchen table. He was a large, powerful man whose power lent him an authority that was rarely challenged, except by my tiny, tireless grandmother. The love between them was the most profound I have ever seen. When I was with them I felt their love fold round me. I think I was happiest there. There is something of my grandfather in Angel. I am occasionally aware of wanting to reach out to Angel the way I reached out for my grandfather.

My grandfather's work clothes were blue overalls. Over those he wore a half-length black coat of a thick, stiff cloth. On his head he wore a peaked cap with a shiny brim. He carried his flask of tea and sandwiches in a canvas bag. Together we would walk the short distance to catch the workmen's early bus. The twelve-hour factory shifts in the town began and ended at six. Twice a day the hooters would signal the shift changes. My grandfather would greet and be greeted by the men queuing at the stop. This was done with great economy of expression. All of them would be carrying rolled newspapers, most would be smoking. The red coals of the untipped cigarettes glowed when the men drew on them. In the wind or rain or snow, the cigarettes would be clenched between thumb and first finger and protected by the palm of the hand. My grandfather's hand, and therefore mine, smelt of nicotine and smoke. His brand was Park Drive.

The real moment of this memory comes on entering the engine shed. The shed was high enough to harbour the night in its eaves. Sometimes birds got in too. There was little light – just a few oil lamps, placed around the sleepers – miserly smudges of orange. And at the centre, the huge dull black of the sleeping engines, steam escaping with an impatient hiss from pistons and boiler. My memory always failed to warn me of their size. Like elephants and steamships, railway locomotives define hugeness because their size is only measurable in units greater than the human scale. The skyscrapers of New York are less impressive – just men and women standing on each others' shoulders until they touch the sky.

By the time my grandfather reached the shed, the locomotive would already have been warmed. The steam-raiser would have lit the fire and checked the boiler three or four hours before. My grandfather would attend to his duties while the fireman dropped into the pit beneath the engine with his oil can. And I would watch and listen to the steam escaping from the valves and pistons, the creak of metal as it warmed and expanded, the crack of coal in the fire box. Then his strong hands would lift me onto the footplate, the brake would be released and the engine would move towards the doors of the shed until it came to rest again at the signal. Beyond the signal, the permanent way: iron tracks catching the lantern light. Further away, the near canopies of the long mainline station, pools of white light along the platform. Here my grandfather would permit a smile. It was a similar smile to the one I saw on Angel's face the day Michael walked in with his head shaved.

6. Michael's Hair – 2

FOR A DAY or so after having his hair shaved off, Michael said he had ideas coming out of his ears. He couldn't write fast enough to get them all down. Finally Angel pulled the girl off the front desk to stand at his shoulder and take dictation. She filled four or five notebooks. I stood and watched as he talked and paced.

'OK. OK. This a TV commercial. For the sports car open top. OK. Desert, middle of the day, big blue, beautiful, blue, aquamarine sky. Huge sky. Maybe a few cactuses around to give the shot a sense of scale, or a . . . I don't know, prairie dog or something walking across, left to right. Big heat. In the distance, through the shimmer of the haze a plume of dust: dust kicked up by a car moving fast along a desert road. So: sky, desert, horizontals, cactus trees, verticals and a cone of dust progressing right to left, filling the screen, chalking it in. Cut to a State Trooper straddling a bike, a Harley Davidson Electra Glide or something, whatever it is they ride. This guy has big forearms, burned brown, crisp shirt, good creases, good jaw-line, a day or so's stubble, no sweat on the man, clean mirror shades reflecting the desert. We see the cone of dust reflected in his shades. He reaches down, lazy, like a gunslinger, turns the key, the engine chokes into life. Nothing on the soundtrack until then except slide guitar, Ry Cooder or somebody else. The next Ry Cooder. Then – BLAT! – the car kicks past. It's there. It's gone. Before the cop can even get the bike off its stand. Dust settles. Gunslinger defeated. He doesn't even try. Cut to the dust reflected in his shades. Then cut to the car's rear-view mirror. A young woman's eyes. Blonde fringe. Just long enough to register and recognise. OK, the pay-off. Front door of a two-room apartment. Wood floors, sparse. Door opens, cop comes in, throws down his helmet and shades onto the couch. Goes into kitchen. Woman at the stove. Line of dialogue from her: "Good day?" He opens fridge. Gets out a beer. The woman turns toward us, it's the driver of the sports car. She goes to the window – the car's there, out the back, gleaming. Secret smile . . . You're looking at my hair.'

'Excuse me?' This is Chester, Angel's sole black appointee, leaning against the corner of a desk: pecs showing through his white, half-sleeved shirt, creases in his khakis, contemporary stubble. Subliminally Michael has transposed Chester into his TV ad and turned him into the trooper.

'You're looking at my hair.'

'You have no hair. How is it that I can be looking at your hair?' Chester doesn't have much hair himself. It's razored very close to his skull. We don't know much about Chester except that he acts as our barometer of cool and seems to regard the rest of us as deeply uncool. I sense his impatience when we talk. His eyes are always swinging round the room looking to fix on something else. Michael says he thinks we despise him for his colour. Michael and Chester don't get on. They frequently row. There's a rivalry between them. Michael is five years older than Chester and he suspects that Angel is paying Chester more. This is not true but I don't feel like it's my place to put him straight.

Chester is a good man. He proved that to me in many ways after Susan's death. Somehow he was the one who moved in to the apartment for a few days, slept on the couch, answered the phone, took Jordan out. And when the voices kept pricking at my nerves like pins he told the people to go away. Then, just as quickly as he arrived, he was gone and it was like all those late-night conversations didn't mean anything. His aftershave hung round the apartment for weeks.

'You're looking at my scalp.' Michael runs a palm defensively over it. Chester looks at me and laughs the way he does when he wants to needle Michael. 'Why don't you just ask me what I think?'

'Why should I care?'

'I don't know. Why *should* you care? You tell me, Michael.'

'Look,' Michael says, 'it's not that I have no respect for your opinions. I would hate for you to think that.'

Chester feigns innocence. 'So why should I think that?'

'You should not think that. You should absolutely not think that. However, my hair . . .'

'Your scalp.'

'. . . My hair is a different issue. Isn't it, John?'

'In terms of?'

'In terms of its . . . significance to the agency.'

That one had us both beaten. Chester said, 'Are you not sleeping, Michael?'

'Yes.'

Chester walked away.

'Why do you ask that?' Michael has a smile on his face to prove he is not angry with Chester – even though he is. He is also anticipating a joke from Chester and he wants to be ready for it.

'No reason.' Chester sits at his screen and picks up the phone, dials, swings his feet onto the desk.

'Why did he ask if I was sleeping?' Michael turns to me, looking desperate now. Chester's still watching him even though he is now in conversation with somebody on the telephone. 'Chester?'

Chester shakes his head. Michael's smile sets hard. He walks up to Chester's desk and cuts the line. Chester's attention fixes on Michael's hand on the phone cradle. He nods gently, swings his feet off the desk and hands the receiver to Michael. 'That is not the action of a rational man.'

Angel's door opens. I don't know how long he has been watching through his window.

'I . . .' Michael turns to me again for an explanation only he can give.

Angel says, 'You want to step into my office?' He goes back inside. Michael follows him in. The door closes.

'That is not the action of a man who is getting enough sleep,' Chester says, picking up the phone again. 'Hi . . . No, Michael cut the line . . . yeah, the guy who shaved his head.'

In terms of a chronology, Michael shaving his head comes later than the Christmas Rosa threw up in the restaurant, but before Susan was killed. This is the order the memories select themselves and this is why I am now thinking of Henry and Maude. Maybe I'll call them tonight.

7. Leona – 2

FOUR HOURS AFTER the telescope conversation I arrived at Susan's apartment. The first thing I did when she answered the door was to hand her photograph back. 'Leona,' I said.

She waited a moment before challenging it with an, 'I'm sorry?'

Susan was always more knowing than me. Whether she actually knew more than me didn't matter. I always felt like she was playing with me.

'Angel said the photograph was of a woman called Leona.'

'Why don't you come in.'

There was a bowl of green olives on the low ethnic table. The walls (brick, unrendered) were painted white and the canvases, all unframed, were lit by downlighters. Predictably, Susan's apartment was tasteful and minimalist. The windows were high and undraped, the floor was American white oak, a light wood kitchen area with dull flashes of brushed steel had been built into the corner of the room and, in pride of place, a Barcelona lounge chair: a few thousand dollars' worth of Mies van der Rohe.

I chose the portrait of the city to stare at. A woman was standing in the window of the apartment opposite staring back at me. Five floors below, the cabs queued in the street. Overhead the sky was clear except for a few clouds which looked like puffs of artillery smoke.

Susan poured two glasses of white wine from the bottle on the counter, came over and handed one to me. I watched her in profile as she drank. She was wearing her slut-red lipstick. It marked the glass.

She said, 'Don't stare.'

'I can't help it.'

Susan should have been a singer: she had Nico eyes, strong bones in her face which vectored down to meet her jaw. She dressed in simple, beautifully cut dresses, usually black, usually knee-length or above. Cotton or linen. She had a number of these.

'Tell me about this painting.' She had turned her back to the window and was looking at the largest canvas on her wall.

'Tell you what?'

'Just tell me.'

'Is this a test?'

She shrugged. I took a step nearer to it.

'No. From here.'

I stepped back. 'Who did it?'

'No questions.'

The painting, needless to say, was abstract. Some abstract art provokes an immediate reaction – fires off all kinds of images in my head – most doesn't. This one fell into the latter category. There was more canvas on show than paint and the little paint there was had been applied in the hallmark fashion of the avant-garde charlatan.

'Any response is valid,' she said, mocking.

'I'm afraid I have no response.'

'Anger?'

'Not even that.'

She lost interest in the game and swung round to face me. 'Why did you steal the photograph?'

'I didn't steal it, I . . .'

'For the period of time the photograph was out of my possession it was stolen. You could argue that after you made the call to me this afternoon it became simply appropriated. Until that point in time a court of law would consider it . . .' She delivered this in a flat monotone, as if she was just going through the paces.

'Do you have some kind of legal training?'

'No. No legal training. My father worked for Boeing.'

'Boeing?'

'We lived in Bellflower. Los Angeles.'

'I see.'

'What do you see?'

'Nothing.'

Susan sat on the sofa and stretched out her perfect legs. I did not sit beside her even though I judged that was what she wanted me to do. 'Tell me why you said that.'

'I don't know.'

She let it go. 'Everybody in Bellflower worked for airplane companies. It was like you were part of this group of people who worked and socialised and belonged together and you got everything you needed from it. You learned to live within boundaries. People who do that, well . . .'

'Do you live alone?' I said.

'Yes. I live alone. I was going to say, the thought just struck me, that if you live within boundaries maybe you develop an appreciation of what you need to hang on those walls to make them more bearable.'

'Have you always lived alone?'

'Always. No. Not always. I lived the first seventeen years of my life with my mother and father. No. Wait. I lived for

33

fifteen years with my mother and father and then two years with my father.'

'Your mother died?'

'Did she?'

'It was a question.'

'Will you please sit down. If you do not wish to sit beside me please sit on that chair there.' She pointed to the Mies van der Rohe. I sat down. She said, 'Tell me how my mother died.'

It went on like this for some time. After an hour of it I told Susan I was leaving. When she asked me why, I told her I felt I was being cross-examined. She said other people had made this observation. I apologised for being unoriginal and she told me not to apologise, originality is rare – and then she laughed and called for Angela to come out. The door beside the kitchen opened and a woman came into the room.

'This is Angela,' Susan said.

'Hello, John Wayne,' Angela said.

The world is split between those that make a joke about my name and those that don't. She didn't so she fell into the significantly smaller, but more interesting category. She was carrying a dinky handgun which she slipped into her purse. Angela is small and intense. She dresses like a Native American which she is not. She does not shave beneath her arms. Her lower and upper jaws look like they come from a different set: the lower jaw is strong and bovine, the top one is smaller. She has thick straw-coloured hair which looks like it's strong enough to pull a tractor.

She took my hand and held it in hers which was soft, moist and limp. It felt like she was taking my pulse. Then she said, 'I should leave now.' Susan smiled, stood and walked Angela to the door. She kissed her cheek and whispered something.

Susan leaned against the door after she closed it. She said, 'I'll explain.'

'I'd like that.'

Susan poured another drink for herself, took my glass, filled it, and took them both over to the sofa. This time I sat beside her.

'But I should be disappointed in you if you didn't already know.'

'About why Angela was here?'

'Yes.'

'Because you thought I might be some kind of pervert?'

'You can never be too sure.'

'So what convinced you I wasn't?'

'I'm not. But I'm a little drunk now and when I drink I find I am less certain than when I'm sober that . . . I want to live.' She went to the stereo and put on some Patti Smith.

'So don't drink.'

'I like to drink.' Susan watched the stylus surf the grooves of the vinyl.

'I'm surprised you're not in a relationship,' I said.

'Why do you assume that?'

'I don't know. I don't get the sense that there's anybody else around. Is there?'

'Not now.'

'But there was?'

'No. I'm a virgin . . . what do you think?'

'I think you're pissed off and I'm not sure if it's me or just the way you are.'

'If we're going to spend any more time together, John, you'll have to take me for what I am.' This was delivered with quite deadly seriousness.

'All right.'

'I don't like glibness. It pisses me off. But I do like to

laugh. And I like people who surprise me. And I have a very strictly defined moral code.'

'Defined as?'

'Another time. And I don't, by and large, like ugly people. I know this is indefensible but aesthetics are important to me. I can't bear to spend time with ugly people.'

'Is that it?'

'No. I don't like people who let me get away with statements like that.'

'Are you interested to know what I want?'

'Not yet. I want to know if you find my terms acceptable.'

Shortly afterwards I left. I didn't hear from Susan for a month and then I called her and we arranged to meet again. That time we slept together and she got pregnant and nine months later Jordan was born.

It was discussed at the trial whether the wound in Susan's body could have been self-administered. Certainly the handgun had her fingerprints on it. But much was made of the fact that a suicide customarily shoots his or herself in the head or in the mouth. Susan died from a gunshot wound to her heart.

8. Meet Jordan

HURTING PEOPLE IS easy but the hurt gets soaked up by the ocean of humanity. This is what Chester and I were discussing two weeks after Susan's death. It was late, after midnight. Jordan was asleep, Chester was lounging on the sofa. I was sitting on the wooden floor leaning against the heavy low table. At the centre of it, a bottle of Johnny Walker Black Label. We were smoking grass, some of the ash was in the upturned whisky cap. A stranger walking into the room might have questioned who the bereaved was. The floor was cluttered with comic books. Jordan was reading through his entire collection – a project he had begun the morning I told him his mother was dead.

'It's like, I don't know, pollution or something.' Chester took another drink and another draw on the reefer.

'Pollution?'

'In a lake – a lake of . . . health. The more people get hurt, the more polluted the lake gets. Then the fish start dying. Then the plant life. Then everything starts mutating so that new lifeforms grow – ones that can survive the new conditions. New York now is kids growing up seeing violence as a way of life: using it for themselves . . . polluted lake of the city.'

I looked over at Jordan's comics. 'Do you think a kid killed Susan?'

'I don't believe so.' He blew an O of smoke. It hung and twisted into a helix and crumbled.

'Why do you say that? Do you think I killed her?'

'No. I don't believe you killed her.'

'I'm interested. I'm interested in who you think might have killed her.'

'Well maybe a kid killed her. I don't know.'

Like Susan, when Chester's shutters came down there was nothing you could do to get them open again. Like Susan's, they were closed for much of the time. Susan's world had a secret door to it. A few people had the key: Angela, a couple of other women, Jordan, perhaps another man. Not me.

Why was Chester there? Why, after knowing him for three or four years, drinking a few beers together but never taking it further than that, did Chester turn up at our/my apartment, two weeks after her murder? And why, when he came, did I start to believe that he knew Susan better than I did? I raised the question with him. He said, 'It's just your perception.'

'Correct. That *is* my perception. That is why I'm raising it with you.'

'What I'm saying is that your perception is wrong. I didn't know Susan. OK. I did know Susan but I did not know Susan particularly well.'

'So why do I feel that you do. Did?'

'Because you're looking round for a reason for her death. Not for the murder. A bigger reason. A metaphysical reason.'

'I still don't . . .'

'No. There's a better reason.'

'For her death?'

'For you thinking I knew your wife better than . . . No. I can't say it.'

'Say it.'

'I can't say it.' Chester shuffled along the sofa, leaned over and stubbed out his joint in the whisky cap.

'Say it.'

'OK. I'll say it. It's about your self-esteem. You don't believe you deserved her so you're creating this scenario in your head in which other people are closer to her than you were. The truth is, you'll never know.'

Chester had a knack of getting close to the truth. He claimed to have the lowest IQ in his college year, but he said he made up for it because he was intuitive and intuition is the most useful kind of intelligence there is. I suppose I suspected that Susan married me only because she got pregnant and she always said she'd never bring a child into the world who didn't have a full set of parents. Our marriage formalised that but the suspicion never left me that if Jordan hadn't come along, we wouldn't have lasted. One night, a year or so into our marriage, I asked her if she loved me. I needed to hear her say she did. She said I played her on a lower scale to the other people in her life.

'Why did you come, Chester?' Because of the grass and the Scotch, time was moving slowly and the question seemed to have been formulated an hour or so before.

'If you want me to go, just say the word.'

'I don't want that. I just want to know why you came.'

'You needed me to come.'

'Yes. I needed you to come. That does not explain why you came.'

'It does.'

When Chester left and, like I said, his aftershave hung round the apartment for a few days, I started to believe I had smelt it before. That when I found Susan's body I could already smell it in the room. I didn't mention this to the police and after a while I couldn't decide what to believe.

That's what happens. After a death it doesn't matter what is true and what is not – it's what you choose to remember of a person that keeps them alive. When homicide gets stamped on the ledger of a life certain details are set in stone: transcripts of the trial, evidence, statements, but these just relate to a brief moment and often even these details are wrong. I find what I remember, and therefore know, of Susan, changes as time goes on. This is what my grandfather believed eternal life was. Not that we live forever, but we live forever in memory and memory gets more and more diluted the further and further down the generations it travels. Soon we're just a speck in Chester's lake of poisoned humanity.

After Chester stubbed out his reefer, he went to piss. I forgot to tell him not to flush because Jordan always wakes when you do. It's OK later in the night, but for the first few hours you have to pussyfoot around. So when Chester came back in, Jordan was following him, except Jordan was asleep. He looked round the room as if he'd lost something. His cheeks were red. He has his mother's features – more evident as adolescence approaches – and is sometimes mistaken for a girl, which he does not appreciate. His fair hair was sticking up. He kneeled down on the floor and started looking under his comic books. I didn't want to wake him so I put my arm on his shoulder and led him out of the room. Chester stood there, not moving, a little concerned. Jordan muttered something in the language sleepwalkers use and walked past him. I guided him into bed and pulled up the sheets. He rolled over onto his side and said something else. His temperature was high. I felt his forehead. He ground his teeth but he looked OK.

Angela came along when Jordan was born. Susan didn't ask whether I minded. Why should I mind? But I was surprised when we got to the hospital to find her there, waiting for us in one of the bright corridors. By the end of it I was grateful. Susan was in labour for twenty-two hours and Angela stayed with her all that time. She fought off the doctors when they said Susan needed a caesarean. She fought off the nurse when she said she needed pain relief. It was a pact they had made. The opposite of a suicide pact. Each promised the other that when they gave birth they'd be there fighting off the chemical squad. It was while I was outside, watching the day break, smoking my first cigarette in five years, that Jordan was born. Angela was holding him when I went back in.

'Do you want to see?' she said, holding the bloody lump of life towards me, wrapped in a green cloth.

'No. I want to hold him.'

The way they looked at me made me feel it was an unreasonable request. Later I apologised to Angela for raising my voice at her.

9. Me and Jordan go on a Trip – 1

THE SUMMER AFTER Susan was murdered somebody said I should take Jordan on a trip. There wasn't enough work to go round at the agency so I asked Jordan if he wanted to go to the Cape for a few days. I told him we could stay with Mrs Lomax and see Henry and Maude but he said he'd found it hard the last time with Henry looking at him like he was responsible for Newton's death. Instead, Jordan decided he wanted to go camping and catch some fish. I think he'd been watching too much Disney.

'So where do you want to go?' I asked him.

Jordan was watching the TV, lying on the couch. He said, 'Somewhere in a camper,' and I knew what he meant. It didn't matter where we went, just so long as it was away.

So I hired a VW Camper van and an L.L. Bean tent. Bought two flashlights and one oil lamp for emergencies. Stocked up on canned tuna. Borrowed two cots. Went to my favourite store and bought a case of beer, three bottles of Johnny Walker Black label and a map (this is why it is my favourite store: nowhere else would you find a good road map and a good Scotch under one roof). I was coming out onto Wooster Street, box of beer, bag of Scotch, maps under my arm when a man fell into step.

'Let me help you there.' The figure reached to take the case. I stepped away and backed up against the wall of an apartment building. It said NO MENUS in a dirty window.

I looked at the man: a good-looking Italian with greased-back hair, a grey jacket in a nice material, long pointed sideburns and empathetic eyes. He was thirty or so years old.

I said, 'Hello, Ray.'

'Let me help you there?'

'Thanks.' He took the maps and the bag of Scotch. He didn't look inside the bag.

Detective Ray D'Angelo lives in Bay Ridge, Brooklyn and worked in the First Precinct bureau. On the night of Susan's murder, Ray walked into the apartment pinning an NYPD gold crest onto his jacket. He was with another detective. The beat cops treated him with respect, the other man they ignored. Ray went straight into a huddle with the officers in the corner of the room. He kept looking up and shooting glances over at me then he came over and shook my hand, offering his commiserations for my loss. As we talked he pulled on a pair of white gloves and started frisking the bedroom. He told me he was working on a move to the South Brooklyn Homicide Squad and he was expecting to hear about the transfer any day now. It seems surreal now, conducting a conversation with a stranger who was fingering through your possessions, flash bulbs going, people coming in and out and a woman on the bed lying under a white sheet that looked like the Japanese flag. The red sun got bigger and bigger as the night wore on. When they turned Susan over the exit wound made it look like a cone of her back had been pulled out like a plug. Something inside her came loose and fell away (there were all sorts of colours inside her). And all the time Ray was working I was talking to him; asking what he thought of Mayor Giuliani (fine, he said, now he's calling for an end to parole), making jokes

43

about his job: talk, talk, talk. I hated myself for that afterwards.

After half an hour or an hour Ray asked me if I had a friend I could call. I said not at 4 a.m. He said a real friend wouldn't mind under these circumstances. I told him there was nobody who immediately came to mind. He took off his white gloves and led me back into the lounge. One of the beat cops had been sitting on the sofa with the other detective watching the TV. They stood up when Ray came in but they left the TV switched on. Ray told them to find some Scotch for me and unleashed some other message with his eyes. The detective seemed to understand it. I didn't. Ray went back into the bedroom.

When dawn broke I looked in on Jordan – this was shortly before they removed Susan's body – but he was sound asleep. When the ambulance took her away Ray and I stood outside on the street watching the fleet of vans coming round the corner from the bakery. He offered me a cigarette and I took one and as we smoked he talked about the procedure and I appreciated him taking the time. Ray told me that this was the part of his job he hated the most: trying to find reasons for people who'd lost somebody they loved. I must have been asking him for reasons, but I don't remember. All I know is that Detective Ray D'Angelo was very human and I appreciated it. Then he said we should go down to the precinct house so he could take a statement. He didn't want to but it was somehow necessary.

When we got there I told him that I'd been with Angel, working late at the agency, and he seemed to accept it but said he'd need to check it with Angel. He asked me who I thought did it and I told him I had no idea. All of it felt very routine; Ray asking questions, walking up and down the small hot room in his shirt sleeves, me answering them. After a while he stopped pacing and, as if the question had been

44

prompted by something, looked hard at me and said, 'Did you love your wife?'

'Of course. Why do you ask?'

'I don't know.'

'Of course I loved her.'

'I'm sorry if the question offended you.'

'That's OK.'

He touched my shoulder then let his hand fall away. 'You get some sleep. I'll be in touch.'

All of this, of course, after I'd woken Jordan and broken the news to him. How do you tell an eleven-year-old boy he'll never see his mother again? I don't know. I just knew it would be easier in the long term if I gave it to him straight and didn't try and offer any false hope. Susan wasn't in the emergency room. They weren't fighting for her life. She was dead so that's what I said to Jordan.

He didn't cry or throw up or scream. He just looked like somebody whose face had been pushed into a freezer cabinet and whose expression had solidified. I asked and asked whether he was all right and he kept saying he was. I tried to reach over and hold him but he just lay there staring with that awful dread look at the ceiling. Everything I said he agreed with. Perhaps you should get dressed: yes. Eat some breakfast: I will. Take a shower: soon.

I called the only mother whose number I could find in Susan's diary and told her what had happened. I asked her if Jordan could come round while Ray took me to the station. Perhaps the fact of it had already become familiar to me, perhaps I should have broken it more gently to her, but she reacted with anger – as if I was somehow responsible for ruining her week with the awful news. Then she cried. After that she apologised and said Jordan could come round for as long as I needed and she'd keep her son at home so he had some company. When she started telling me how she'd have to call work and explain why she wouldn't be in I put the phone down. I didn't need to hear any more details.

'Party?' Ray said.

'No. I'm taking Jordan camping.'

'They give you a discount on the beer?'

'Just stocking up.'

'See, I never do that. Stocking up. I buy and I consume. That way I don't get into habits.' Ray smiled. 'We need to talk.'

'Not now.'

'OK. When?'

'Soon.'

'You said soon last time.'

'Soon. I promise.'

'Why not now?'

He backed off when he saw I wasn't going to shift. I'd known him a year by then and we knew each other pretty well.

He said, 'You call me.'

'Yes.'

'Yeah?'

'Yes.'

'You call me.' He hooked the bag over my fingers, put the maps on top of the beer case and crossed the street. Halfway over he pulled up his collar. On the other side he turned away down an alley.

I shivered off the thought because if you don't think it you don't have to confront it and if you don't do that then it's not real. Who killed Susan? This is what Ray wanted to talk to me about because Ray had a hunch it wasn't the person who was currently in prison serving fifteen years for what the criminal code calls voluntary manslaughter.

★

We drove out of the city on Friday morning, stayed overnight in hotels, drove on during the day. Jordan read comics and played with the electronic game Chester had bought him the previous Christmas. I listened to the radio. The silence between us became so unbearable I'd stop for gas just so that I could talk to somebody. Eventually we arrived at a town called Cody. By then we'd shared sufficient words to agree that we'd be satisfied if we found a lake, hired some rods and did some fishing. Neither Jordan nor I had ever fished before but he said there would be people around who'd show us. Maybe we needed a task to bring us closer together.

Cody is a rodeo town. It's named after Buffalo Bill – William Cody – and it trades on the association. There's a rodeo in a huge arena most nights and Jordan said he wanted to go, so we booked into a motel on the outskirts for the night and headed into town for something to eat. This wasn't what I'd envisaged when we set out on the trip: I'd expected birdsong, foxes in the wild, huge still lakes, not a town full of men in cowboy boots.

I called Carol from a booth in the café while Jordan read the two-foot-high laminated menu. We spoke at prearranged times. She picked it up at the first ring: 'John?'

'Hi. We made it to Cody.'

There was a Jordan-length silence.

'John . . .'

'What's wrong?'

'I think Steve knows about us.'

'Where is he?'

'Now? I don't know. It doesn't matter where Steve is now. I think he knows about us.'

I looked over at Jordan giving his order to a woman. She had a pad on a piece of string tied to her belt, tight slacks, a 1950s blouse and hairstyle but she was dressed too young for her age. Jordan pointed towards me. She looked over and dropped the pad. It swung on the string.

'Wait a second, Carol.' I held my hand over the receiver and squeezed the concertina door open. I called, 'You order for me.'

Jordan looked up as if he didn't understand, even though I knew he did. The waitress relayed the message. Jordan picked up the menu again and disappeared behind it: just his fingers showing round the side. The waitress was smiling at him now. She'd fallen in love with him the way people do.

'I'm sorry, Carol. I was just asking Jordan to order up some food for me.'

'What is the matter with you? I just told you Steve knows about us and all you can talk about is Jordan ordering your food.'

'Right. I'm sorry.'

'So what do we do?'

'Do?'

'About Steve.'

'Oh, Steve. I don't think there's anything we can do about Steve. Don't speculate. Just ask him what's wrong.'

'Is that wise?'

'Who knows?'

'And what if he says he knows?'

'Then we'll just have to deal with it.'

'No. I'll just have to deal with it.'

'Whatever.'

Carol sighed. 'You're not being very supportive of me, John.'

Jordan laid down the menu again and started mouthing something at me. I mouthed back that I didn't understand.

'. . . John?'

'Just one more second, Carol.' I squeezed the door open

again. The slats folded in on themselves. The wood was thin, like balsa. I called, 'What?'

'Can I have a beer?' Jordan shouted across the room.

'No you cannot have a beer. Order me a beer.'

Jordan smiled up at the waitress. Then shouted: 'A root beer!' The waitress laughed. I think she was simple. I closed the door again. The waitress wrote something else on her pad. The manager was looking over at her: a fat Italian man in a white shirt standing behind the counter. His hair was greased flat but it was curly. The curls were fighting clear of the grease at the fringe and over the tops of his ears.

'Jordan wants a beer,' I told Carol, wanting to share the preciousness. I'd forgotten for a second that she wasn't Susan. 'Carol?'

'John. I think I should just tell you that I am extremely angry with you. However, I do not like arguing on the telephone. But I feel it's important that at least I let you know this.'

'I'm sorry. You were saying that you think Steve knows about us?'

'Yes.'

'So leave him.'

'And live where? With you and Jordan? I don't think that would be a very good idea. Do you?'

'We could try it.'

'John. Whatever my needs are at the present, however angry I feel, I can still appreciate that you and Jordan do not need me in the apartment with you.'

'No. Maybe you're right.'

'Are you OK?'

'I'm fine.'

'You sound a little . . . vague.'

'Just tired.'

The waitress swung her hips as she walked to the counter.

49

Jordan was slyly looking at her ass. She slapped the order down and the fat manager took it, scanned it, then passed it into the hatch. His hand came out empty. He looked at the waitress, she smiled at him to show she didn't care how much he stared, picked up a pot of coffee and went down the line of men on the stools, filling their cups. The manager eyed her slopping the coffee into the saucers.

Carol had been saying something for a while. All I heard was, 'John, are you still there?'

'I'm still here.'

'Are you not listening to me?'

'Of course I'm listening.'

'So tell me something nice. Leave me with something to get through tomorrow.'

Jordan had turned the menu into a tent on the table. He was putting the condiments inside, reaching deep into it. Salt, pepper, mustard. Father. Mother. Child. Why I thought that I don't know, but I know he thought it too, which is why, at that point, he looked over at me with a huge weight of sadness in his eyes.

'. . . John?'

'Something nice?'

'Yes.'

'Look, Carol. I have to go.'

'OK. So leave me to remember that. That I called you and you didn't want to know.'

'That is not true. Not true.'

'Goodbye, John.'

'I'll call tomorrow. Same time.'

'Suit yourself.'

'Carol?'

But she was gone.

I went over and stood by the table. I didn't want to sit down in case he needed me to hold him. Several people had said that Jordan would probably cry about Susan, but something else would trigger it off. A year after her death he was still holding it in.

'Are you OK?' I said.

When Jordan looked up he had that stupid smile back on his face. He knew what this was about. It seemed the only way he could show his pain was to hurt me and he knew what hurt me most was him denying he felt anything at all for his mother. I do that sometimes. Sometimes I make people need me so I can freeze them out and show them I don't need them. I needed Carol but that night I wanted to make her feel like I didn't.

'I ordered you a hamburger with cheese,' Jordan said.

'Any salad?'

'No.'

I sat down. 'And what did you order for yourself?'

'A steak.'

'. . . You didn't think to order me a steak?'

'I ordered you a hamburger with cheese.' He looked over at the waitress and smiled. She winked at him.

'Don't play with the condiments.'

He slapped the menu flat. The salt and pepper pots fell over. The menu sprung up again, back to its tent shape.

'I told you – don't play with the condiments.'

He righted the salt pot then picked it up, poured some into his palm and licked it. I reached over and smacked him on the side of his face. He didn't dodge my hand which is what I'd expected so the contact was harder than I intended. Jordan's hand went up to his ear. He looked defiantly at me. I never hit Jordan. Maybe once or twice, but mainly never. The waitress came over and stood protectively over him. Jordan got up and pushed past her. He was nearly her height. He walked quickly through the restaurant and out onto the main street.

'Two steaks.' The manager slid two plates loaded with hefty steaks down the counter towards the waitress. Jordan had ordered one for me after all. The burger was a joke – like the root beer. He'd cooked it up with the simple waitress, they had the same mental age. I took off after him.

Outside, the traffic was building up for the nightly rodeo. Four-wheel drives carrying families and dogs, bikes on racks mounted on the back, were queuing to park, the men bantering good-naturedly to each other through car windows. Two hundred years before, similar men would have been circling their wagons for the night. I couldn't see Jordan so I went back to the camper. I left the door open to let out the heat that was sealed inside. Jordan turned up an hour later.

He said, 'I need some money.'

'How much?'

'Thirteen dollars.'

I gave it to him and he trooped off again. A few minutes later he came back, stepping a little bouncier. He climbed into the passenger seat and reached in the glove box for his Gameboy.

'Any change?'

He pulled two dollars out of his Levis.

'No, you keep it . . . look, I'm sorry.'

'I had to pay for your steak. He made me pay.' Jordan kept his concentration fixed on the game.

'You went back to the restaurant?'

'I was looking for you.' The game bleeped.

'You didn't think to come back to the van?'

'I guess I didn't.'

'So what did you do? You went back to the restaurant?'

'Yeah.'

'Straight away?'

'No. I walked around. Then I went back to the

restaurant.' Jordan put the game down. 'Do we have to go to the rodeo?'

'Not if you don't want to.'

We cancelled the motel and drove out of town. That night we parked up by the Shoshone river and took out the tent. It took us an hour or so to get it up right, but it was worth it for our first night under the stars. Jordan was asleep as soon as he lay down on the cot. I went and stood by the river for a while, then I took off my shoes and socks and stepped in the icy water. The current tugged at me, trying to make me fall. The numbness spread up my legs to my knees. I stepped in a little further, feeling the stones on the soles of my feet. The canyon reached up high towards the sky. I looked above the shadow of it at the stars and thought about Jordan. I wondered if Susan kissed him goodnight the night she was murdered. Seeing that look on my son's face in the café made me realise how important it was to get him to talk. There are things that harden inside you if they don't get aired.

10. Chinese Angel

O NE NIGHT NOT long after Susan and I met, I was working late at the office. It was after ten and the only other person still there was Angel. I prefer to work when the phones are switched off and Michael and Chester aren't arguing, and when the Spanish woman who brings the basket with the strange-tasting salt beef sandwiches isn't hanging around for hours talking to the girl on the desk, but really eyeing up Chester. The only thing that makes it hard is the guilt. Angel always leaves the office last so if you stay late, he does too. On these occasions what he does is order in some Chinese food and Thai beer from his favourite restaurant on Hudson Street then he calls you into his office to share it. Your part of the ritual is to feign both surprise and delight that he has gone to the trouble. You also have to offer to pay. Sometimes he lets you so there is a real negotiation taking place.

You get a half-hour warning of the food arriving because Angel orders it by shouting down the phone at Lap, the owner's son. He shouts because he thinks Lap is stupid and can't speak English. The problem is that Angel orders the dishes in Chinese – which he can't speak so well. So at around 9.30 you hear the sound go down on his TV and, if you're watching him through the glass wall of his office, see him pull out his glasses from his shirt pocket, get the phone book out from his desk drawer, turn on the desk lamp with the green glass shade, lick his finger to turn the pages, then squint under the bottom of his glasses at the phone to dial, and through his glasses to read off the number. Don't ask him why he doesn't set up the number on his phone memory, or write the number down on a post-it, because he won't tell you. He'll just keep saying 'Why?' or 'So what?' So the first time you go: 'Because it'll save time.' 'Why?' 'Because you don't have to look up the number.' 'So what?' 'Because looking up a telephone number is a waste of time.' 'Why?' 'Well, you can use the time for something else.' 'What?' And so on. Just another of Angel's rituals.

At 21.18 by the red digits of the ticker on the building opposite (Dow Jones up 83.45 points, external temperature + 11) I heard him on the phone. 'Lap, take this down . . . You know who this is. You don't need my number. Take this order down with your pencil . . . And tell your father hello from me and he is also a very dear friend and much valued friend. Do you have your pencil, Lap? That's good. OK. I should like Siu Jyu yuk. Did you get that? Siu Jyu yuk. Yes? . . . And a Cha Siu Bao . . . Lap? Are you still there, only I thought I heard the line go dead? OK. Now, how about some Mai fun. Mai fun, right? Lots of fun . . . No, Lap, I was making a joke. Lots of fun. Not lots. No, sufficient for two people . . . Well, if your father wants to put a little extra fun in then who am I to tell him not to? . . . OK. Tell me how much you charge for the Har Gow, I want to check we're reading off the same list . . . How much? Yes, that's what it says on mine . . . OK. And some Thai beer. Four bottles. You want you can read that back to me . . .'

We ate the Chinese food from cartons on Angel's desk. The small TV was on in the corner of his office. Angel's walls are blocked out with family photographs: his nephew Harry, and Harry's wife and child. All fat. His father, Hershel, sitting on a bench in Central Park in the 1920s before he got fat, arm thrown over the back which makes me think the photograph was taken by a woman and she'd just stood up, but he'd left his arm in the same place. Behind him there's very little traffic on Fifth Avenue and the street looks like some of the buildings have been weeded out.

In the centre of Angel's wall there's a very tattered sepia photograph of his father's younger brother's family. Seven children standing, neatly graded like Russian dolls, and one in the woman's arms. She's sitting side on to a low *chaise-longue*, giving the camera an even stare. There's a big-leafed plant behind them on a narrow, high table draped with a white cloth. The man is standing with one hand on the woman's shoulder. He looks tough, like a soldier, he has a stiff collar and long coat. It's a proper studio portrait and it was taken in Kiev in 1934. What gives the photograph significance is that in 1941 over thirty thousand Jews were murdered there, this entire family was among them. I'm sure the story is familiar to many people, but I hadn't heard it when Angel told it to me.

He said, 'My father heard about it from various sources. September that year all of the Jews in the city are called to assemble. They're told they're going to be resettled. Of course rumours had been reaching them of atrocities, but they were just rumours. And when they assemble they're told to undress. All of them: women, children, men. A machine-gun bullet for the woman trying to cover her shame, but for the rest of it – silence . . . And then they're marched in columns out of the city. Through the streets. Imagine the sight. Thousands of naked people trying to maintain their dignity. Somebody who saw them said what he remembers is the sound of the jackboots on the cobbles and the silence of the bare feet. You ever hear about Babi Yar?'

'No,' I said.

'Babi Yar is a ravine. This is where these good people are taken. In groups they're led to the edge. In groups they're machine-gunned and fall down the ravine. It takes two godless days. Then they set explosives into the walls of the ravine and bury the people who died there . . . Except the earth continues to move. Some of the people are only wounded. Children, women, who knows, trying to climb up through the bodies. Two years later they dig out the earth. Jews are forced to do this. They dig out the earth, pour petrol over the corpses and burn them . . . Now when somebody asks if you heard about Babi Yar you can tell them you have.'

Occasionally Angel tries something new. Once he made the mistake of ordering Mexican from a menu somebody left at the desk. His tongue got tangled in the unfamiliar words. 'Tamales – am I pronouncing this correctly? – Tamales. Yes, I believe I just said that. And a side order of Frijoles . . . No, I did not ask you to repeat that back to me. No, I asked you the first time, not the second. I have a very good ear for language on account of extensive travel round Europe both during and also just after the last war . . . and you have just lost a customer. Yes and goodnight to you, fuck.'

After we'd finished the Chinese food and Angel had taken the cartons out to dump them with the garbage on the street he opened us a second bottle of beer each.

'You know that kid, Lap?' he said.

'Yes.'

'I don't trust him. I think he's pissing into my food.'

'I don't think so.'

'You don't think it tasted . . . pissy?'

'No, Angel.'

'I catch that Chink fuck pissing into my food I'll have his balls cut off.'

We used to get through three or four girls on the desk a year. Chester told me that he met one of them in a club one night and she seemed angry at him. Finally he got it out of her. She said we all knew what Angel was like with women so why didn't we protect her from him, or warn her at the very least? Chester told her he didn't know what she was talking about. She said that Angel would come up behind her while she was working and slide an arm round so he could touch her breasts. The first time she thought it was a mistake. The second time she slapped his hand. The third time it happened she was alone with him in the office and she was frightened. He trapped her against the wall and unzipped himself. Told her to touch his dick. She tried to push him away but Angel is very strong and he just held her there and panted in her face. She said she should have grabbed his balls and pulled hard but she didn't know how he'd react so she felt she had no choice but to oblige him. She reported him to the police. Nothing came of it. Angel has some powerful friends. A new girl started two days later.

Angel lives in a brownstone in Gramercy Park. He is hugely rich and it's said that he holds incredible parties there. Ray told me that some of the precinct commanders are regulars and that a couple of times the ambulance was called because a girl got hurt. He said I didn't want to know how she got hurt but Fatty Arbuckle's name was mentioned by the EMS team. It wasn't the men at Angel's parties that concerned Ray, it was the women: not the hookers, the guests. And all the time they were guests of Angel's he gave them a mask and a name and for the duration of the party they were allowed only to use that name. The mask was optional.

Rituals.

Ask Angel about his rituals, in a roundabout way of course, and he'll say that ritual is what gives life meaning. See a person without rituals, you see an unhappy person. Then he'll mention Babi Yar and he'll fall silent. Somehow he ties the two thoughts together. Angel's mind is a strange place to be.

11. Virginia Woolf

SUSAN DIDN'T MIND me working late. Sometimes I wished she did. Even after Jordan was born and I expected her to need me around to help, she didn't. Often Angela would come round and when I got back, sometimes after midnight, they'd be there, talking together: huddled on the sofa, listening to Courtney Pine or Miles Davis or some folkie Angela had heard at Lilith Fair and they'd be whispering so they didn't wake Jordan. They had this thing about not using the lights so Angela would bring scented candles and they would place them round the room and I'd spend the weekend chipping the coloured wax off the wooden floor with a knife.

For a long time I suspected Susan and Angela were lovers. It wasn't anything concrete, just the physical proximity they seemed to need. Angela would touch Susan's hair all the time, run her fingers up her bare arms. I suppose Angela thought I'd taken Susan away from her, but when I knew more about Susan I came to understand that intimacy and friendship meant the same things to her. Once she let somebody in they got everything. I couldn't help but find it threatening, but at least it was easier to bear because it ended up being about her needs and not mine.

Susan and I shared a belief that the relationships that survive are the ones in which both parties agree to maintain a respective distance between each other. Most other couples I know seem closer than Susan and I were, but neither of us could bear close proximity for long. I know Angela found this hard to understand. I heard Susan explaining to her one night that she'd prefer to have somebody like me to move towards than somebody who was in her face all the time, so the only option was to back off. This is how I felt too, but it took Susan's explanation to focus it for me. Angela once called me a shithead and said I'd do anything Susan asked of me because I was weak. For once, I defended myself without resorting to abuse, which was its own kind of victory.

Susan read a lot of books. Pretty much what you'd expect, you'd find on her shelves, and a few others. Marilyn French, Kate Millet, Anaïs Nin, Colette, Renee Vivien, Camille Paglia, Alice B. Toklas, Joan Nestle, Sylvia Plath, Virginia Woolf, Martha Gellhorn. Dyke fiction, she called it, disparaging it before I had the chance to, even though I never would. She said she went through what she called a 'LibFem' phase when she first met Angela. I asked her what differentiated this from the other Fems that were on offer. She said it was the least radical because LibFems allow that men can change. She had a particular passion for Virginia Woolf: her novels, her diaries, her essays, anything she could get her hands on. When I told her I'd visited the house she was living in when she died she begged me to take her. Susan hadn't visited England before so it seemed like a good idea to go over for a few weeks in the summer. She was three months pregnant then and wanted to travel while she still had the chance. I wanted us to stay for a while with some of my family, but she didn't. I said she showed no curiosity about my family. She argued that was because she had no curiosity about them. If it was a brother or sister or father or mother, then fine, but as I possessed none of these, just an aged grandfather, an aunt and a few cousins here and there she said she'd rather stay in hotels. I told her we could stay in hotels if she wanted, but whether she liked it or not, I was at least going to call in on my grandfather. He was eighty-nine at this time, I hadn't seen him in five years and I didn't expect him to be around for much longer. Then, inevitably, Angela's name came up. It seemed she'd expressed an interest in joining us on the trip. The argument went on for two weeks. Susan won it by saying that if Angela didn't come I might as well go on my own. Then Angela decided she didn't want to come on her own because she'd feel 'left out' so she asked if she could bring along the moron she was seeing at the time: Carl. Carl looked like a Nazi beach bum with crew-cut fair hair, a long neck and Aryan hard blue eyes. He was tall, thin and muscular and wore sneakers and shorts. Shorts on a man repulse me and the prospect of having to look at Carl's legs for three weeks nearly decided me to cancel the whole trip. I'm glad I didn't.

The flight arrived at Gatwick five hours late. We hired a Ford Granada and packed our bags in the trunk. The plan was to spend a few days in London then go down to the coast to see Virginia Woolf's house and afterwards to drive north and see my grandfather. Angela and Carl would then bail out for a week to allow Susan and me to spend some time alone. That was the plan. So, after four days of visiting galleries and trying to find the heart of London and failing, we drove down to Sussex.

The afternoon before that, Angela said, 'Has Susan told you about her mother yet?'

'What about her mother?'

We were on a café terrace in Covent Garden. Susan was walking round the pretty shops with Carl to help him look for something to take back for his daughter who lives with his ex-wife in Boulder Springs. She's cohabiting with the private detective who provided her with the ammunition she needed to end her marriage to the moron.

Angela said, 'What has she told you?'

'Not much.'

Angela narrowed her eyes, trying to work out whether I was telling her the truth. When we were alone together we didn't even try to hide our hostility. When we were with Susan we hid it pretty well because we knew whoever showed it first would lose. Susan would have to side with the other and the whole edifice would crumble.

'Look. Just tell me what you know, John. OK? I'm trying to be nice to you. What is this stuff?' She was eating a thin sandwich. It was garnished.

'Cress.'

'Is it edible?' She wrinkled her nose at it.

'Yes, well no. It's a sort of cross between decoration and food.'

'Why is the bottom of it brown?'

'That's what they grow it in.'

'Shit?'

'No. Just . . . I don't know. Some kind of compost.'

'Miss!'

Angela waved her arm around until the girl who served us came out to the terrace.

'I didn't ask for this cress. Take it away, please.'

'You could just leave it,' the girl said.

'Yes. Just leave it,' I said. 'Brush it off.'

She held her plate up. The girl took it away and brought the plate back without the garnish. Probably she'd wiped something on the bread like waitresses do when people piss them off. Angela managed a terse thank you and took a drink of her weak tea. Angela is allergic to dairy so the tea was black, the sandwich was tuna (no spread). She was also vegetarian but not vegan. She didn't usually eat fish but she made an exception on the trip because she was afraid she wasn't getting enough protein. I suggested peanuts but apparently they make her fit. At least she's afraid they'll make her fit because of what she's read. They don't. I crushed some up and put them in a veggie lasagne once when she came round for supper. She was OK. Susan told me Angela's menstrual cycle was messed up and she put this down to English food. Why this pleased me I don't know.

I said, 'All I know is what she's told me.' We were still talking about Susan's mother.

'OK. And . . . ?'

'And she told me she didn't come to the wedding because she doesn't get along with Susan's father.'

'She told you that?'

'Yes. Is that not true?'

'No. That is quite categorically not true.'

At this point Carl came back because he'd lost Susan. He hadn't found a gift for his daughter, Grace, but he had found a shop which sold 'cool boots' so he'd bought himself a pair. He opened up the box and started lacing up a pair of Doc Martens. The smell of leather and polish swamped us.

The next day we drove down to Sussex. We stopped twice because Susan thought she was going to throw up. She didn't, but she looked white and stressed. When she got back in the car and I asked her if everything was OK she pulled away as if her car sickness was my fault because I was driving. In the back Carl was nodding to Steely Dan with his Walkman wound up high. I heard, 'Aja, when all my dime dancing is through. I run to you.' Angela was pretending to be interested in the landscape but straining to hear our conversation in the front. The discord between Susan and me pleased her. Occasionally she shuffled up to Carl and laid her hand on his knee just so she could show me the smug look in her eyes in the rear-view mirror.

I asked Susan if there was anything I could do for her. She pulled her vintage Levi jacket tight around her and glared at the fields. Then she picked up the map, turned it round and said, 'Turn here.' It was a mark of her intelligence, her incredible map-reading ability. I said, 'Which way?'

'Right.'

So I turned and soon we were cruising past a garden centre with a big car park and a number of stooped, grey-haired people pushing low metal trolleys of tall foliage. Beyond a short row of ugly houses was the sweep and fold of the Downs and the distant corduroy of ploughed fields. I switched on the radio. Susan sighed and hunched closer to the door. I asked her again if she was OK. Angela chipped in that we should be nearly there. Suddenly she'd decided to help diffuse the tension in the car. Carl, of course, was completely unaware of it. 'Hey. Did you see that!' he said, screwing his head round to watch a huge bird take flight from the side of the road.

'What was it?' Angela said.

'An albatross,' Susan said, even though her eyes were closed.

Carl said, 'You didn't see it. How did you know it was a bird?'

'I just knew.'

Carl hummed the 'Outer Limits' theme and Angela smiled.

Suddenly, Susan said, 'Let me out!' and shouldered the door open. I hit the brakes and we stopped before I had a chance to look in the rear-view mirror. Susan got out of the car. Me and Angela and Carl sat for a moment watching her as she walked away from us. I opened my door. Angela said, 'No. I'll do this.'

Carl and I watched her approach Susan, ask her something, touch her arm. Susan shouted something violent because Angela pulled back a little before regaining her composure and taking Susan's hand. Then she held her and turned her away from us so we couldn't see her crying.

'Chicks,' Carl said, sagely. He wound down the window and lit up a malodorous hand-rolled cigarette.

'Smoke that outside,' I said.

So Carl got out too and stood behind the car. We were parked beside a tall hedge. In the wing mirror I could see him jumping up and down to try and see over it into the field. Susan and Angela were talking more calmly. For a second I thought I might turn the key and drive away from these people and never go back to New York again.

'Hey.' Carl had crept up on the blind side and now he was leaning in to my window.

'What?'

'I guess you should know that Susan's mother killed herself . . . Angela told me not to tell you. That's all I know, thought you should too.' Carl patted me on the shoulder and stood up straight. The window framed his taut midriff: a pale T-shirt with a washed-out Budweiser logo on it. In the circumstances our destination suddenly became hugely inappropriate. Not just Virginia Woolf's house, but the place she was living when she committed suicide. Carl leaned in again, his face leering through the window. 'Slit her wrists.' He watched it sink in before moving away and kicking out his cigarette. Then he reached down and picked something out of the hedgerow. He held up a speckled blue bird's egg.

'For Grace,' he called and came back for the second time. 'I just had this idea. I'll get her something every place we go. That way it'll be like she was with me.' He reached into his pocket for his tobacco tin and set the fragile egg on a nest of Golden Virginia. 'Maybe I'll hatch a phoenix,' he said.

We parked in a gravel car park close to the house. Nobody was saying much. Susan got out first and headed off up the narrow lane. Angela and Carl waited for me to get out next, then followed at a short distance. Carl lit up another cigarette, Angela asked him if it was necessary for him to do this each time he got out of a car or a building, Carl said that it was since it was now illegal to smoke inside any confined spaces. Then he mused whether smoking in the fresh air was in some way healthier than inhaling smoke indoors. Angela was beginning to answer just as I stooped through the low door of Virginia Woolf's house.

The first room was full of people in walking boots and windcheaters: ruddy-faced, late-middle-aged types with maps in plastic envelopes and unnecessary compasses. Those who were talking whispered like they were in church. The floor was stone. The furniture was probably once painted in bright primary colours. Now it was faded. The house has been comprehensively trashed by the Bloomsbury set. There are photographs of Woolf with her husband and E.M. Forster and Lytton Strachey and T.S. Eliot. Starchy, buttoned-up men, puffed out with their own self-importance. The photographs are intended to make you feel some connection with the house. For me it worked the other way round. I would rather have just seen the house and filled in the gaps myself.

I wanted to see the bathroom but they wouldn't let me. I asked the man at the door in the white shirt and tartan tie what he thought of Virginia Woolf's suicide and he said he had no opinion. I asked him why there was no mention of it in the pamphlet he gave me when I walked in. He said that the house was a testament to her life, not her death (but he was making this up – all credit to him). I told him that many people remembered her because of her death. He said the work spoke for itself. I said that for me, and I knew for Susan, the most interesting fact about her was that she killed herself so dispassionately. I mean, she decided to do it because she knew she was breaking down again and she couldn't bear it. So she left a note for her husband then walked down the lane to the edge of the village and took the farm track along the flood plain to the river. She must have contemplated drowning herself for the fifteen/twenty-minute duration of the walk. She must have been so sure.

The man's patience ran out so I went outside the back of the house looking for Susan. The sky was clouding over with the kind of menace you only feel when you're away from a city: a full palette of swirling greys. The garden is vast. From the lane the house looks small, but behind it the lawn and flower beds extend to an acre or so. On the edge of the garden is a church which crouches, ready to pounce, beyond the top fence. A couple of formal gardens claim the space by the conservatory. Away from the house is a wooden shed where Woolf wrote. Carl was staring in and a woman in an orange windcheater was standing beside him. He was explaining his plan of collecting something for his daughter, Grace, everywhere he went. The woman was smiling in the kind of absent way you do when you're talking to someone you think might just pull a knife on you.

When I reached them she was saying, 'I couldn't write in there, could you?' in a voice that must have carried to the back of school halls. A lanky man with binoculars stumbled up the grassy slope to her. When he reached her she said, 'I couldn't write in there.' As if the thought was worth uttering once, never mind twice.

'In there?' he said, and peered in at the spartan desk and candle and inkwell. 'No. I couldn't write in there.'

Carl started telling him he was collecting something for his daughter, Grace, everywhere he went, that way, etc., etc.

I went back inside to look for Susan. Angela was in Virginia Woolf's bedroom: a newer building tacked on to the side of the house. It felt like a sick room. I asked her where Susan was and she said she thought she was with me. Then I got a feeling that answered most of the questions I'd been asking myself that day: Why are we coming here? Why is Susan saying she's not depressed any more when I know she's been feeling like killing herself since she found out she was pregnant? Why didn't she tell me about her mother? The answer: She'd thought it through and she'd arrived at a similar conclusion to that of her literary heroine.

I ran back through the house, Carl was sitting on a bench by the conservatory. He said something as I passed him but I didn't quite hear. He had a small unremarkable pebble on his knee which he was looking at as he ran his tongue along the gum of another Rizla paper.

I jogged back down the lane to the car park. Then I slowed down to a walk. Suddenly, inexplicably, I wanted to savour this. I abandoned Susan to fate. I could not save her, I knew this now. And I wanted to know what Virginia Woolf felt when the madness was on her again. I wanted to feel the knife-sharp wind cutting through me as it cut through her as she set off along the farm track, through the small copse of trees then out into the open: the tall mounds of the riverbank, nearly a quarter of a mile ahead. And all around her the open plain; wide and featureless with the grass blasted to crystal by the wind and a few sheep grazing.

The sheets of my sanity blew in the breeze.

I saw Susan ahead of me, walking resolutely on. I dropped my pace to match hers. She stopped at a five-bar gate, unlatched it, and its weight swung it slowly wide. She pulled it closed behind her. I think she saw me but she carried on as if she hadn't. I followed her. We walked like this for ten minutes more before she reached the riverbank and climbed up. She stood at the top and I could see what she felt about the river by the way she stood. She leant a little forward, just testing the breeze. I looked away. I couldn't bear to watch.

When I looked back she was gone.

It took me a minute or so to run to the grass mound of the bank and clamber the fifteen feet up it. When I reached the top I stood in awe of the woman who had chosen to drown herself here. This was no genteel current, no sun-warmed flow. This was a brutal swollen rush towards the sea: a wide screaming tide of muddy water running from the land, barely constrained by the banks. Nothing could stand in its way. No one would last in it. I looked right to the sea framed in the U of the white cliffs. I looked left towards the town with the castle standing above it on a hill: like a chess-board with a game in progress and one of the rooks dominating the board.

Then I saw Susan. She had walked along the blind side of the bank and now she was sitting on the damp grass just watching the river. She was holding her denim jacket round her, drawing all of the comfort from it that she could. I climbed down and sat beside her.

'I just want to think about her without feeling angry,' she said as if I could grant her this wish. I put my arm around her and she rested against me. We talked for half an hour about her mother then we went back to the car.

Carl and Angela were waiting inside. Carl had a stash of mementoes on his knee: a dusty twig, a cigarette butt, two pebbles, a chocolate wrapper. He was writing labels for each of them in tiny script on a piece of white paper. Angela saw us holding hands and there was real hate in her eyes. When we got in she didn't say anything. As we drove away Susan covered my hand with hers and I felt something flowing between us as if each of us had opened a vein then pressed the wounds together allowing our blood to mingle.

12. The American Cockroach

I WAS TALKING to Angel about Jordan and what I'd caught him doing one morning when I got up. Jordan always woke before me. When Susan was alive he'd come into our bedroom and make enough noise to wake one or both of us. Then he'd commando up the channel between our bodies and get into bed between us. Usually he'd lie against Susan and she'd put her arm round him. This died down as he got past six or seven, but he still did it some weekends. The bed was always full of crumbs from his breakfast. Susan and Jordan had some kind of telepathic connection. If he was ill she'd wake in the night a moment before he did. If he hurt himself at school she'd know before he got home. It wasn't an exhibitionist's kind of love they had, she'd rarely touch him in public, but it was a steel bond that linked them. One other thing I remember thinking recently is that they rarely smiled when they were together. The way they looked at each other went deep, deep inside: a moment that looked like vacancy from each of them during which they seemed to vacuum up each other's thoughts before they could go on. After Susan was murdered Jordan came into my bed once but said it didn't feel right so he stopped doing it. He'd just sit and watch TV until I crawled out and fixed breakfast for him. I was drinking too much so getting out of bed was a chore.

Something Susan and I often talked about was that Jordan should be encouraged to tidy his room, fix his own food occasionally, put his laundry in the basket. A boy his age should be capable of doing these things. Jordan seemed incapable of doing any of them even though (maybe even because) he knew it would provoke Susan's anger. All of the attempts to make him more self-sufficient stopped when she died. I went to a support group to try and get some advice but for an hour and a half all they seemed interested in doing was talking about how awful it was for them. I just wanted to forget it and find some new rules so we could move on. But there are no developmental rules for children who have had a parent torn brutally from them. Unless, of course, you try to forget that the awful thing has happened and you apply the same ones that you did before. Then you feel guilty all the time because you think you should be compensating the child for the loss. Life is tough enough on them without making it any harder by giving them a hard time about their bedroom not being tidy.

I tried to raise this at the group of tired-looking people (in a dingy, tall brown building zedded with fire escapes). After I'd introduced myself and told my story and everybody had made the right noises, I said, 'I should like some rules.'

Eva Something, the 'facilitator', took it upon herself to translate for me. I sat down (having previously stood up to talk like an alcoholic at an AA meeting – 'My name is John Wayne and my wife was murdered'). 'John asks if there are any rules. I wonder can anybody help him on that one? Yes, Jan?'

Jan looked like the dark-haired girl in the 'Scooby Doo' cartoon. Her husband had been shot dead in a car park one night for the thirty-five dollars in his wallet. 'I think, John, you should rely on your instincts. You should not feel guilty about asking your son to help around the apartment. You should recognise that you have needs too, and one of those needs is time and space to examine what you are feeling.' She smiled.

An untidy man bundled in. His name was George. 'I see it this way. When my wife was taken I felt I had to be everything to my daughter: everything that her mother was to her. I twisted myself into being some person I wasn't. And soon she didn't know who she was dealing with. Before, I used to scream at her . . . and then, when I stopped, she started pushing me harder and harder. Doing things that were entirely unacceptable. And I just smiled and smiled . . . until one day I snapped and screamed again . . .' He looked round the group and decided we needed the moral spelling out. 'And after that it was OK.' George sat down. The man next to him squeezed his arm. Then he stood up, a thin academic type in a dusty tweed jacket. He made his points by pointing his pipe stem.

'I've been reading up about this. It's a similar situation to that of adoptive parents. Children's behaviour is, at times, unacceptable. Adoptive parents have to get past the stage of questioning whether the behaviour is rooted in their child's sense of abandonment. The point is that you can't second guess the reasons or you'll go crazy. Just deal with it as it comes.'

'I suppose what Edmund is saying,' the facilitator was on her feet again, 'is not to try to censor your own emotions. Don't ask – no, I shouldn't say "don't", forgive me. It is unhelpful to both you and the child for the bereavement to cloud your natural parenting skills. If your son is behaving inappropriately then discuss this with him. If he says to you, "Mom would have understood, or forgiven," then you are perfectly within your rights to say, "Yes, maybe Mom would have forgiven. But Mom is no longer here. And I cannot countenance that behaviour." Jan?'

Jan smiled. 'And, John, you should know that we're all here for you. We understand what you're going through. We have been through it ourselves and we all came through. Is that right?'

People nodded, a woman Amened, George clapped. We broke for coffee or, Eva told us, if we wished, we could contribute towards the bottle of red wine that Edmund had been kind enough to bring along with him.

I mentioned to Angel my hunch that support groups are part of the Disneyfication of American culture. If you can find a reason that makes sense of what has happened to you then you can draw some kind of moral from it. That takes away the awful pointlessness of it. Morals are the crutches agnostics use in the absence of a bible to turn to. Morality is the lingua franca of mainstream American culture which is why so much fuss gets made when writers or film-makers get charged with portraying something immoral. Their defence is usually that deep down they're profoundly moral but to illustrate this best they just had to show something that wasn't. This makes it very hard to be truly immoral nowadays because there's a danger you'll get fêted for being truthful and brave. In truth it's very hard being at all bad because another part of this Disneyfication is that bad people are victims too and we should understand and forgive. You won't find many victims of crime sharing this view.

When I got up one morning and found Jordan in the kitchen toasting a cockroach, Eva's words came into my mind. I said, groggily, 'I cannot countenance that behaviour.'

There was an empty bottle of Jack Daniels on the drainer.

Jordan ignored me and tried to turn the creature with a fork. He'd tied it to the grill pan with a piece of fuse wire so it couldn't get away. He had to untwist it before he could flip the insect onto its back.

'Jordan.'

'What?' He burned his finger on the pan and cursed.

'What are you doing?'

'What does it look like?'

Morning is no time for a battle of wills so I let him get on with it and made some real coffee. I watched the creature fry. It gave off a smell like burning rubber. First its antennae frizzed and burned off, then the four back legs stopped moving. Finally the forelegs gave out. It was a pathetic sight.

'We have an infestation,' Jordan said. He poured a glass of water over the creature and untwisted the fuse wire. Then he dropped the two-inch husk onto a plate on the table. It chinked like a piece of charcoal.

Everywhere in New York is infested with cockroaches. Now they tell us that the rat population is also reaching epidemic proportions. But cockroaches really repulse me. When you turn on the light at night you can see them scatter. They disappear so fast that you feel you've been hallucinating.

'This is an American cockroach,' Jordan said, prodding the thing with his fork. 'It's lighter in colour than the Oriental cockroach and bigger than the German cockroach.' He went to his room and brought back a book which he started reading from. '*Periplaneta americana*. Adult roaches live for approximately two years. Their egg case contains approximately fourteen eggs. Nymphs emerge in about one to two months and undergo thirteen moults over a period of six to twelve months. They are known as born inebriates . . .'

'Thank you. That is sufficient information.'

'We have to eradicate them.'

'We will.'

He paraphrased: 'It's estimated that the female German

cockroach (not the American, they're slower) will produce four to eight egg cases in her lifetime. That's around three hundred babies. In sixty days these babies will be having babies of their own. If half of these are females and each produces three hundred nymphs and so on, from one German female cockroach you could get more than one hundred thousand cockroaches in your home by the end of the year.'

I took my coffee cup into the bathroom and turned on the shower. Jordan followed me and sat on the tub with his book. I removed my robe. He looked up at my unfamiliar nakedness, briefly interested, then back at his book.

'We need to find where they live. Set traps.'

I stepped into the shower. Jordan was still talking but the sound of the water drowned out his voice. When I turned off the tap and reached for a towel, he said, 'Is that OK?'

'Pass me the towel.' Since Susan stopped doing the laundry the towels felt scratchy. 'Is what OK?'

'That you buy some traps.'

'Yes. That's OK.'

American cockroaches like the heat. No surprises there. They thrive in boiler rooms, around hot pipes, under tubs and around radiators. Jordan was convinced they were coming up from their HQ in the basement boiler room to raid our apartment so we should go down there and check it out.

'We'll do that,' I said.

'I'll get my flashlight.'

'Whoa. Not now.'

'Why not now?'

'I've just had a shower and . . .'

'And your head hurts and you can't face eating breakfast. OK. You just kill yourself too, then.' Jordan walked out, leaving his book on the floor.

'. . . If you feel that strongly about it we'll go now,' I shouted after him.

There was a pause, then he said, 'I'll get my flashlight.'

'I cannot countenance that behaviour,' I said under my breath.

The boiler room is next to the laundry room in the basement of the block. The basement is humid and low lit and every so often you can feel the vibration of the subway through the concrete floor. Jordan led the way into the laundry room with his flashlight. One of the big dryers was churning a load of candy-striped sheets but nobody was down there.

'So?' I said. 'What do you want to do?'

'Look in the boiler room.'

'Are you sure?'

'That's where they'll be.'

'And what if they are?'

'Then we know where to set the traps.'

'Lead the way.'

We went out into the narrow, stifling corridor. Off to the right was a storeroom full of chests and crates, at the end was the metal door that led to the boilers. The air hummed with electricity, a wide pipe flushed above our heads, the corridor was garlanded with thick cobwebs, everywhere smelt of detergent. Jordan stopped in front of the door.

'You open it, I'll get ready with my flashlight.' His bravado had failed him. He stepped aside. I took the metal handle and twisted it. The door gave a little. I yanked it open, Jordan jumped in front of me and turned on the flashlight. The black mass on the floor shrunk and the floor turned pale again.

'Shi . . .' I said.

'I told you,' Jordan said queasily.

'So . . . are you going to go in?'

'Are you?'

'Follow me, partner.'

I stepped in and switched on the light. The room lost its menace. An old-fashioned boiler dominated the space. It looked homey and reassuring. Jordan walked around it but he didn't stoop into the shadows where the pipes went through the walls, or look too hard underneath. We were both aware of being watched by thousands of evil little eyes, both sensed being sensed.

'Dad,' Jordan said.

'Yes?'

'I'd like it if you didn't drink so much.'

'Right.'

'You could just try.'

'I promise.'

'So you've stopped drinking?' Angel said after I'd finished telling him all this. He was eating Sushi from a black plastic tray.

'Virtually dry when Jordan's around.'

'My friend in the mayor's office says eating Sushi is like going down on a corpse.'

'Yes?'

Angel wiped his mouth. 'And when Jordan is not around?' His voice was phlegmy from the food.

'It doesn't matter. Just as long as he doesn't see. That's all that matters.'

Angel didn't disagree.

Two weeks later (six months or so by now after Susan's death) I called Eva the support woman's number. Her ansaphone was on and her honeyed voice invited me to leave a message. By the time she called back I'd drunk far too much.

'Eva, I should like you to answer me a question.'

'If I can do that, I surely will.'

'Why would you fuck somebody and then shoot them dead?'

'I'm sorry?'

'Answer the question.'

'I don't know, John. I'm afraid I can't answer that question.'

'You see, what I didn't say at the group . . . What I didn't share with you was the truth . . . the reason she was murdered. Not the reason. Just one of the tricky details . . . yes?'

'Go on.'

'I found a condom by the bed. By the body. In a saucer. A condom. Used . . . and I hid it so the police wouldn't find it but Ray . . . the detective . . . Ray made me go through it all when he took me down to the station house that morning. He made me feel ashamed and so I had to take him back to the apartment to show him where I hid it . . . Eva?'

'Yes, John.'

'Do you understand what I'm saying?'

'Yes.'

'I don't use condoms, Eva.'

'John, can you let me have your address, please.'

'Why do you want my address?'

'I sense you shouldn't be alone right now.'

I gave it to her. Then I got worried that she'd pass it on to Edmund or one of the other happy bereavees. I called her back to warn her not to but I got the machine again. When the door buzzer went I was glad it was her. She looked at me professionally before she stepped through the door.

'Can I get you a drink?' I took her jacket, stumbled, and caught the couch to stop myself falling. 'What time is it?'

'One thirty. I'll do it.' She pointed towards the kitchenette, throwing a question mark by raising her eyebrows.

'Go ahead.'

She went over and opened the refrigerator, knelt down a little so she could see right to the back.

'Sorry about the mess,' I called out, seeing the carnage of the apartment through her eyes. The wood floor was gluey with dirt. It made your soles cling to it when you walked across it.

'Have you eaten?' She pulled something out of the refrigerator and looked for somewhere to throw it away. The pail was full and stank. Jordan and I had performed an exorcism on it the day before but neither of us felt like clearing it out.

'Yes. I've eaten.' Then I thought about it. 'Well, not today. But this week I've eaten.'

Everything she heard and saw seemed to make her more concerned.

'And your son. Has he eaten?'

I couldn't help her with that one. I expected he had because I gave him money to eat. I assumed he spent it on food but I didn't feel it was my place to go round checking up on him.

'Sit down,' she said. She took my arm and steered me to the couch.

'Now. Why don't you tell me what kind of support you're getting.'

The next time I went to the group I tried harder. I sat next to my new friends, George and Edmund. They pulled apart and made space for me to sit between them. Edmund went to fetch me a cup of bad coffee from the machine. George said a lot of reassuring things. I felt the weight of support from them both when it came to my turn ('My name is John Wayne and my wife was murdered'). Within five or six visits I was just as good as the rest of them. Whenever anybody new came it gave us all an opportunity of telling them about our pain. When people got tired of doing this they left and more people came. More and more. There are a lot of hurt people around.

The majority of the people I've met in my life have been good people. Maybe that sounds like too big a generalisation. I don't think it is. I think people are born good and life is an assault course we have to get through. Every obstacle tests our innate goodness. What surprises me most is how few people fail the course. The problem is that the people who run the news networks are only interested in those people so it's those you hear about the most.

Perhaps I went to the group to look for a reason to live beyond Jordan. I asked Eva if this was a good sign. She thought about it, then said, 'Yes, John, it is. Congratulate yourself for having taken an important step on the road to wellness.'

13. Theme Bars

I USED TO meet Carol in The Library, one of the newer downtown theme bars. Nowadays a bar is not a bar unless it has a theme. As you might expect, The Library is decked out as a study with wood-panelled walls, thick books and old-fashioned card catalogues. We liked it. The whole point of bars like these is to flatter your vanity. Irony is the newest thing in New York City. You drink in theme bars because you get the joke. Everybody else does too but somehow you're made to feel that they don't. We tried Idlewild once, which is themed as the interior of an old Boeing, but Carol said it made her feel air sick. Susan's father would have been appalled by it.

Carol is an 'older woman'. She's forty-six years old and has been married to Steve Gil for twenty-two years. From the outside the childless marriage looked solid until we met. People find Carol spiky. She doesn't try the usual trick of flattering people with a friendliness she does not feel. I suppose she's a true New Yorker in that she's only really happy when the city has wound her up to fever pitch. Anything less, however much she says she craves it, is being only half alive. Steve Gil works in education. He started as a teacher and he's now one of the city's district superintendents. Carol talks about his job sometimes but I tune out when she does. I know, and she knows, that she does it when she feels guilty about us. I make a pretence of listening to help her out. That way, we can feel civilised and grown up about the affair. If I told her the truth – that I had no interest in him whatsoever – she'd have to defend him to me and then we'd have a ridiculous argument about the merits of somebody we were both betraying. I listened long enough to know that he's been involved in some project to make the children of New York more literate, i.e. to teach them how to read and write in English, which a remarkably small percentage of them seem capable of doing.

I stood next to him at a party once. He was telling an impressed southern matron (she had a neck like a turkey and lots of gold jewellery): 'In a city of something like two hundred languages or dialects, literacy inevitably is a problem.'

'I'm sure it is,' the lady said, feigning interest.

'I mean, nearly fifty per cent of children in grades one, two and three are enrolled in the project.'

'I'm sorry. The project?'

'Project Read.'

'Yes. I see.'

'Which is an extraordinary figure when you consider it,' Steve prompted.

'Extraordinary.'

The hostess came up and steered them smilingly apart. What the matron was wishing was that she was forty years younger. I suppose Steve Gil was too. He was wearing a grey suit and, under it, an extraordinarily patterned waistcoat and a Mickey Mouse tie. He's tall, six feet two, and, for the want of a better word to describe him, distinguished (a full head of steel grey hair, portly, very rational). Carol said later she hated seeing him at parties schmoozing people. They thought he was 'Mr Fucking Urbane', while at home he didn't lift a finger. Apparently he thinks the sun shines out of the mayor's ass. He drinks beer all night, surfs the net for hard porn, and blows off all the time. And for such a big man he can't hold his drink. Also his sperm count is low. She really hammered that one in.

'Did you want children?' I asked her.

'Of course.'

'So what are you going to do about it?'

'Be a good aunt. Try not to get bitter. Stay thin.'

The relationship we had was unbalanced. For as long as she was married to Steve I held all the cards. It didn't matter. I felt something for Carol which I didn't even feel for Susan. We could talk about anything. We knew exactly what the other was feeling at all times. We found each other sexually exciting. For me, however, I liked the idea of Carol more than I liked Carol herself. One or two glasses of Scotch, the right song on the radio, and I could picture us lasting forever. The reality was inevitably disappointing.

Carol dresses like Steve, cleanly and expensively. (Labels are important to her: Jil Sander, Dolce and Gabbana, Liz Claiborne and Manolo Blahnik shoes. She slums it in GAP.) She buys expensive underwear. She uses Chanel No. 55 lipstick. She has (again, like Steve) grey hair which she has dyed silver (she used to dye it blonde). It's cut short with a fringe and sideburns like Joanne Woodward's. There's no spare fat on her five-foot-four frame but behind her toned, tanned legs you can see squiggly little blue veins trying to break the surface. She proudly declares to anyone who will listen that she has no cellulite and to maintain this boast she employs a personal trainer at the gym she visits three or four times a week. She freely admits that the trainer is more use to her mental than her physical health. Fabio (deeply toned with erudite musculature and a pony-tail) coerces her, congratulates and flatters her through the programme and when she has finished and her make-up has run and she looks like a forty-six-year-old again he tells her she looks beautiful and she believes him. Italians can get away with this because American women mistakenly believe that Italian men are not so hung up on youth as American men. They are. They just happen to have an accent that makes it harder to tell when they're lying. I said this to Carol once. She said, 'I know when a man like Fabio wants to screw me and when he's being polite. I am still at an age when if I asked Fabio to come home with me I wouldn't have to reach for my chequebook.'

I said something weasely like, 'I'll take your word for it.'

Then she walked out on me which she did quite often.

Carol works in interior design which she argues is no less tautologous than working in advertising. She used to have an office but now she just has a business card and a mobile phone which she always switches off when we meet. Sometimes I wish she'd leave it on because then she wouldn't need to get it out of her purse every five minutes to listen to her messages. She was coming out of a client's party the first night we met. She had refurbished an apartment in the block opposite to mine (ours). Carol says she finds it easier to have sex with me than Steve Gil because I won't feel any less for her if she wants to experiment. I'm sure Steve Gil would be happy to experiment with her too but she says it's hard to feel passion for a man who blows off in his sleep like a whale.

I had to ask, 'How does a whale blow off?'

'Very loudly.'

I was introduced to Steve Gil at the party. Carol didn't know I was going and I didn't know she was going so it was a shock to see her there talking to a man at the far side of the room. The man had a pretty-boy face with dimples and flicky blond hair. Carol was flirting with him, cocking her head back to laugh delightedly at something he was telling her, then nodding vigorously with a newsreadery look when he said something else. I felt betrayed so I decided to ruin her evening for her, but before I could, the hostess steered Steve to face me and the southern woman to a glassy-eyed megaplegic in a wheelchair by the bar.

'Steve Gil.' He held out his hand after transferring his wine into the other one.

'John Wayne.'

He wondered for a while if I was telling him the truth. He must have decided I was. 'English, right?'

'Absolutely. Though I have lived here for nearly fifteen years.'

'Fifteen years?'

'Yes. Nearly.'

He contemplated the period for a while, mentally checking off his material progress. 'So how do you know Carol?'

'I don't,' I said, too quickly.

'You don't know Carol?'

'Carol? No.'

'OK.' He nodded slowly. The hostess came up with a tray of vol-au-vents. We took one each, then she offered a paper plate and Steve, with remarkable sleight of hand, transferred the pastry case to the plate without putting his wine down. How he did it defeated me, but the hostess took my glass while I did the same then handed it back to me with a patient smile.

'Thanks, Carol,' Steve said.

'Oh, Carol,' I said. 'That Carol.'

Steve looked at Carol and then back to me. 'Who did you think I meant?'

'I . . . your wife.'

'No. Not my wife. This pretty lady.' He coiled his wineglass arm round the other Carol and she laughed and shrugged him off and parted a group of people with her tray. 'You don't know Carol?' he said.

'No. I mean I know Carol. But not my wife. Your wife.'

Steve nodded slowly. I took a bite of the vol-au-vent. It was loaded with a pungent, glutinous fish sludge. I swallowed the mouthful without breathing so I didn't have to taste it. 'What do you do, Steve?'

'OK . . .' He squared up like a boxer, preparing to tell.

'Don't tell me. Something to do with the arts?'

'Why do you say that?'

I took a sip of the red wine. It was acidic. 'Your waistcoat,' I said. 'Your waistcoat argues for an artistic temperament.'

He was pleased. 'People tell me that, John. Although my artistic side finds its expression in what many would imagine was a non-artistic job of work.'

'Really? That's interesting.'

'Are you aware of Project Read?'

'No, I'm not.'

'Literacy is a problem. In a city of something like two hundred languages or dialects . . .'

Five minutes later, during which Steve had briefed me on Project Read, I caught Carol's eye across the room. She immediately stopped the man who was talking to her by touching his arm and making a deft apology. She carried a smile across the room with her and stood beside Steve, amplifying the smile at me, just a flash of panic in her eyes, then beaming it towards Steve who was still boring us about his job.

'Introduce us,' Carol said to Steve when he stopped for

breath. She snuggled up to him and he put his arm round her.

'This is John Wayne.' He gestured his glass at me, Carol took my hand. 'Hello, John Wayne.'

'And this is my wife, Carol, who you don't know, ha ha,' Steve said.

'I'm sorry?' Carol said.

'John said he doesn't know you,' Steve smiled at me, trying and failing to make the confusion amusing.

'Steve told me his wife's name was Carol. I mixed you up with that Carol,' I said looking towards the hostess.

'You're very familiar,' Carol said.

'Then maybe we have met.' I directed this one to Steve.

'No. You're being very familiar,' she said, dealing it out with a hard edge to her voice and no smile at all in her eyes.

Steve glossed it over, 'I was just talking to John about Project Read.'

'Were you?' Carol said dryly.

'Fascinating,' I said. 'I never knew there were so many languages – or, indeed, dialects in the city. How many did you say there were, Steve?'

Before Steve could launch into his routine for the third time, Carol cut across. 'Excuse me, John, I hope you won't consider me awfully rude, but I have the most terrible headache.'

'I'm sorry to hear that,' I said.

'I was rather hoping my husband would accompany me home.'

Steve Gil looked at his watch. 'It's 9.30,' he said.

'Yes. I know what the time is.'

'Well, darling . . . it's early.'

'Forget it. I'll go on my own.' Carol pulled away, Steve tried to laugh it off for my benefit. Carol didn't appreciate this. She said, 'What?'

'I'm sorry?'

'What are you laughing at?'

'I . . . I wasn't laughing, Carol.'

I should have walked away. But Carol turned to me and said, 'You saw him laughing.'

'Carol, please . . .' Steve was embarrassed now. There was no way back.

'You saw him.' Punch, punch, Steve and me, both getting it. Me deserving it, Steve not. I was trying to work out who I felt most sorry for, him or her. I decided it was him and I still hadn't forgiven her for being flirty with pretty-boy so I said, 'I don't think Steve was laughing.'

'No?'

'No. I think Steve is embarrassed because you two should be talking about this in private.'

'You're trying to tell me what I should do in private with my husband?' Her voice had risen a tone.

'What you and your husband do in private is . . .'

'Carol, come on . . .' Steve tried to pull her away, but she wouldn't move. Now it was between her and me.

'I didn't ask whether Steve was embarrassed, I asked whether you saw him fucking laugh.'

Carol was drunk. Alcohol twisted her obduracy into intransigence. This was usually a prelude to the self-pity phase.

'I saw Steve smile. He didn't laugh.' I started to walk away.

'You bastard!' I thought she'd screamed it at me, but when I turned round, luckily Steve was getting it. Carol 2 appeared smoothly beside them and put her arm over Carol 1's shoulder. She tried to steer her towards the door. Steve leaned down and whispered something at her, then moved off into the crowd. I circled round the room, and by the time I got back to the door, Carol 1 was shamefacedly taking her coat from Carol 2 and saying goodbye. Steve had been assimilated by a group of men by the bar. They stood in solidarity in a tight scrum, backs to those highly strung creatures they call women (somebody would already be observing that you can't live with 'em and you can't live without 'em, provoking a laugh for Steve's benefit and also to show they were all in it together).

I followed Carol out and caught up with her just as she flagged down a cab.

She said, 'This must not happen again.'

She got into the cab and pulled the door shut behind her. Her coat belt caught in the car door. She turned to look at me through the back window. Her face was very white. When the cab pulled away the belt buckle jangled along the road. I watched her until the cab turned a corner and the narrow street was empty again. Except that empty is a relative term in New York. Even in empty streets you feel you're being watched. Or maybe this is just how I feel.

The next time we saw each other we met in Central Park by the Bow Bridge and headed off slowly in the usual direction. Our route took us along the bank of the lake towards the Boathouse Café where, depending on how long we had, we'd either drink tea and eat blueberry muffins or cut inland and walk down towards Fifth Avenue where we'd part again like strangers. It was raining; a cold chilling rain that found its way down your neck and felt like needles of ice on your hands. The sky was grey, like a scarf pulled up as far as it will go round your face.

Carol said she felt guilty about Steve which I told her was understandable. She said, 'I'm getting old. And I don't want to end up alone.'

'You won't.'

'You don't have the authority to say that. If Steve finds

out about us he'll leave me and find somebody young like everybody else his age does.'

'Not everybody.'

'Everybody. The men in this city tend to stay with their wives until their wives reach the age their mothers were when they first met their wives.'

'. . . Is that true?' I said, when I'd worked out what she was trying to say.

'Then they change them for women who are the age their wives were when they first met.'

'I don't care how old you are. Age is not important to me.' I kissed her to reassure her about my commitment, but also because I felt like it.

'I wasn't talking about you.' Carol looped her arm in mine and our pace slowed. 'But what is important to you?'

'Apart from you?'

'No. The truth.'

'But you are important.'

'OK. So me aside.'

'Jordan. Jordan is very important to me.'

'I mean outside of your responsibilities.'

'I don't see him as . . .'

'You know what I mean.'

We stopped by a damp bench. Carol checked it for bird shit then sat down, pulling me down beside her. The lake was pitted with tiny craters of rain.

'It's not a trick question,' Carol said.

'The truth is, I can't say. No, I need to think about this . . . What is important to me is stability.'

'Stability sounds like a prerequisite of something else.'

'Contentment. Happiness. I don't know.'

'Let yourself go a little.'

'What are you asking?'

'I'm asking what is important to you. That's all. I find it

extraordinary that you can't answer without examining the question from every angle. What is important to you?' She faced away now, angry.

'I can't say.'

'Christ, John.'

She dropped it and we walked on again in silence. I steered us down to the model boat lake which is where I used to take Jordan sometimes on Sundays. Lately he hasn't shown much enthusiasm for it so I have found myself going there alone with a thick pile of Sunday papers and a half bottle of Scotch. The only difference between me and the vagrants is that I read the papers rather than sleep on them, but some days it's a fine line. On this particular day, there were two men by the lake. The more elderly one was silver-haired with a luxurious black coat, circular gold-rimmed glasses, a homburg and a beard. He was steering a U-boat with a toggle on his matt black remote. The boat accelerated and slewed as it turned, cutting circles round an antique yacht which was swanning in sedate ovals. A younger man with a cadaverous face wearing a thick sleeveless jacket and baseball cap was operating this with great concentration. Another cracked obsessive. Ten years older and he'd be marked down as a Vietnam vet. He was sitting on a canvas trestle stool under a green fishing umbrella. Every time the U-boat made a pass and rocked the yacht he sent a broadside stare at the other man to indicate his displeasure. The older man didn't seem to care. Each time his vessel circled it passed closer until the bows almost touched.

I pulled myself back from the place I had been – which was standing on the prow of the yacht.

'I know what you're asking,' I said.

'Do you?' Carol was watching the boats too, but abstractedly. You never see that light in women's eyes when they watch model boats or trains.

'You're asking if I think we'll end up living together.'

'No. Not at all. It's not an option.'

'Because you say it isn't.'

'It just isn't. It wouldn't work.'

'Why do you say that?'

'Because I'd resent the fact that Jordan is your priority and end up hating you – or making you choose between us. Jordan is your Steve, your guilt, but you don't see it.'

Finally the U-boat connected with the yacht and the contact was sufficient to spoil the geometry of the younger man's course. He put down his remote and set off to stride the thirty yards over to the old man. All this was played out on the far side of the lake so we couldn't hear what was being said. The yacht bumped against the mud bank, bounced back a little and the slow current took it away. The obsessive loped in long strides; arms swinging, fierce in his rage. The old man pretended not to notice but his U-boat was patrolling far away from the yacht now, performing intricate figures of eight, startling the sparrows and drowning their song. When the men met, the young man wheeled his arms around angrily pointing towards the lake, the U-boat, the yacht, then jabbing a finger towards the old man's face. The old man just nodded and took it and eventually the anger played itself out. The young man crossed his arms, nodded a few times and shrugged his shoulders. A few minutes later the old man was handing over his remote and the young man was powering the fast boat with abandon.

I said, 'What do you mean Jordan is my Steve, my guilt?'

'If Jordan found out you were seeing somebody he'd react like Steve. Jealousy; hurt; rage. That's what I mean.'

'Every relationship is a long goodbye,' I said.

Carol switched on her interest. Her attention had three settings: neutral (marginally depressed, long sighs and

93

silences), medium (irritable, impatient, angry, occasional bitter laughter) and interested (real or feigned happiness, combative, argumentative). In conversation she would switch between moods, usually her range was two. Occasionally, when the consumption of alcohol was involved, she would widen it to the full three. Today she skipped from one to three. 'Only you would say something like that,' she said.

'It's true. When we meet somebody, we're already preparing ourselves for the separation. That's why relationships don't last. People are always getting ready to bail out.'

'In your experience.'

'That's all the experience I have to go on.'

'Exactly.'

'And death. Life is about getting ready to die.'

'Are you always depressed, John? Because when you say things like this I have to assume you're a deeply depressed individual.'

'I don't think so. How can you tell?'

'You can tell.'

'I'm not.'

'Then get some help. Or get some different experiences.'

Most of the time I was with Carol, if we did talk about our other lives, she tended to dominate the conversation. However, on a recent visit to The Library, she asked me about the night we met, and what exactly happened to Susan. Over vodka and Mexican beers I told her all I knew and then she said, 'Why didn't Jordan wake?'

'Wake?'

'If Susan was shot in the next room then Jordan would have woken − wouldn't he?'

It's a question for which there is only one answer, but it is not a question that was asked at the trial. And if, indeed, Jordan did wake, then by the time I got home he must have seen his mother's body, perhaps also the murderer, and then got back into bed and feigned sleep.

No wonder he took to grilling cockroaches.

14. The Agency – Lunch

ANGEL'S WORKING LIFE began in the family garment business which was started by his father after he came over from Russia in 1903. His old man was a skilled cutter of ladies' garments and soon got caught up in the Jewish Labour Bund which, for vulnerable immigrants like him, provided some economic muscle and also worked hard at protecting its members' cultural roots. Much of Angel's personal and political philosophy derives from his father. The garment trade was heavily unionised and it needed to be. The conditions in the sweatshops were lethal. According to Angel, a blaze in 1911 at the Triangle Shirtwaist Company cost 146 lives which led to a whole raft of long overdue labour laws. He never articulates this as any kind of motive, but the agency is a good place to work: it's light with big windows and good air-conditioning and a very high quality of fittings (Angel's door furniture is symptomatic of this).

Angel's route to where he is now detours round family brushes with the hoods of the 1930s (his father talked about his relationship with the notorious gangster Louis 'Lepke' Buchalter), a move of the company's production out of New York and down to the south-west where the labour was cheaper, and finally a shift away altogether to Taiwan. Angel soon came to realise that however good the clothes were, and they were good, if you didn't advertise, you didn't sell as many. His father believed that quality sold itself. They argued over this and hot-headed Angel walked out. For a week he trudged the grid between Thirty-fourth and Forty-second Streets, Sixth and Eighth avenues, looking for a company willing to pay him to help them tell the American public about their clothing. He drank a lot of coffee in smoke-filled cafés. He side-stepped the push boys on the sidewalks, blinded by their cartloads of garments. All he wanted was one company to offer him the chance to sell. Finally one did, the half-page newspaper advertisement in the *New York Post* got people talking and soon, sure enough, his father was taking the credit for encouraging the boy to go out and make something of himself.

Angel's instincts led him to the Young and Rubicam agency where he studied the copywriting style of one of the best – George Gribbin – a bright young man who'd just joined the agency from Macy. Angel was lucky. The *New York Post* had been bought by Dorothy Schiff and under the editorship of her husband the sombre broadsheet was reinventing itself into a sensationalist tabloid. Angel was born with a tabloid mind so he found writing copy that suited the paper's house style easy. When TV came along not long afterwards, Angel was well placed to exploit the new medium and when he sold out twenty-five years later he owned the seventh biggest advertising agency in the country. The new agency is his hobby. He bought it because he got bored playing golf all day. I think he dreams he'll build it up again and take on his old company, but he doesn't have the hunger any more. His politics remain fiercely and genuinely Democrat. I can say this about few of the people I know. However much people like Michael profess to be Democrats, salami slice them and you'll find they have Republican written all the way through. Angel sneers that they have Democrat hearts, Republican heads.

Angel says that it was while he was walking the Tenderloin looking for work he got a taste for Italian food and he still prefers pasta for lunch; cappelletti or fusilli with a carbonara or Veneziana sauce. If you don't buy your sandwiches from the Spanish woman with the basket, you can go in with his order from Trinelli's, an Italian restaurant in West Thirty-seventh Street. One of us usually sits in with Angel because if he eats alone he spends the rest of the day on everybody's back. So we have a rota: Chester, Michael, Jennifer (who is part-time so the rota is adjusted to take this into account) and me. Much of the information about his family history is promulgated at these long lunch sessions. The stories get embellished. Sometimes Angel reads something and commandeers it as part of his own story. This is how he came to tell of the shoot out between his father and 'Gurrah' Shapiro on Fortieth Street one winter's night. Snow, sedans cornering at speed, men hanging on to running boards, bullets splintering shop fronts, everything.

Chester told me that Jennifer was sitting in with Angel on the day they heard about Susan's murder. I made the call to him because by midday things had calmed down and all Jordan and I were feeling was empty and nauseous. Susan's father was on a flight in from the West Coast and the police were doing what they had to do with the evidence they'd collected at the scene. Ray called to check we'd settled into the hotel and fill me in on the process: 'OK, so we're running DNA tests and also checking the prints on the gun through SAFIS. That way if we get a match on the latents we know who to go calling for.' Ray knew I needed to be told these things. Because I had no answer to the big question, anything I could learn I jumped on. 'And we're running the bullet through Brasscatcher. Sometimes we find the bullet and the gun don't match . . . How are you doing, John?'

'I don't know.'

'We'll get him.'

I remember how I felt when I heard Angel's voice that lunchtime. The girl from the desk put me through even though she said he was in conference. She apologised when I told her who it was. She said she didn't recognise my voice and was I OK because I sounded a little husky?

What I said when I got through was, 'I can't come in, Angel, Susan's been murdered.' I was standing in the centre of the hotel room holding the phone and walking round. The day was ferociously hot and the fan was trying to cool the air but as soon as the propeller swung away the heat mugged you again. Jordan was lying on his bed in the next room. I could see his bare feet through the connecting door. His right foot was beating, his left was still, a sign he was listening to music on his Walkman. There was a big fly buzzing round, looking for food. Every time I thought it was gone it circled round again like in a David Cronenberg film.

Angel didn't say anything straight away. I think if somebody I knew had called me with that kind of information I'd have reacted with a 'No!' or 'You can't be serious!', something inappropriate to reflect the shock. Angel didn't answer, almost as if he'd been waiting for the news.

Then he said, 'I am so sorry, John.'

Then the first flashback. Bed, red sun on the sheet, and the smell of death.

'. . . You take all the time you need.'

'Thanks, I . . .'

'You want I should come over?'

'No . . . no, just. It's OK, Susan's father is flying in and I think we need some time to just . . .'

'Who did it, John? Do we know who did it?'

'No. Not yet. But Ray – the detective – promises me that they will.'

Angel spoke and went on speaking. Jordan came out of his room. He was wearing jeans but no shirt. His ribs poked through his chest, there was no muscle on him. His face was troubled, or puzzled. He saw the fly and jumped for it, trying to catch it in his right hand. It eluded him and flew towards the window. The windows were magnifying the light, penning white blistering rectangles of it on the floor. Jordan stalked the fly and jumped again. His hand moved so fast I didn't see it. When he opened his palm to me it was red and pulpy with a pool of yellow pus at the centre like a lanced boil. He poked at the mess with his other finger, then scraped the carcass down the sink and rinsed his hand under the cold tap.

'Is that Gramps?' he said.

'No. Angel.'

He went back into his room and got back onto his bed.

'John?' Angel again.

'Yes?'

'You let me know if there is anything I can do. Anything.'

'Thanks.'

'Night or day. Anything.'

'Yes.'

'You send the bills to me.'

'Bills?'

'The funeral expenses.'

'Right.'

'You booked the funeral?'

'No.'

'Then you give Leona the send-off she deserves. No. Leave it to me. I'll send somebody.' I heard him tearing off a piece of paper, writing something down. 'John. You listen to me for one minute. Are you listening to me?' The receiver was under his chin now, cradled against his shoulder, strangulating his voice.

'Yes, Angel.'

'You take something from this . . . do you hear me?'

'I can hear you.'

'Make sure that you take something from this. Something my father taught me. Do not turn your head away. Observe it and take something away from it for yourself . . .'

'I can't talk any more.'

'Where are you?'

A man arrived at the hotel an hour later. He had immaculate lush back-swept hair and Liberace smarm, thin briefcase, gold tan and accessories. Angel had sent him. He worked for a funeral company and he talked in a well-modulated voice about the options available to us. We worked out the cost. He was a homosexual. He didn't volunteer the information, but I asked him when I heard his voice and smelt his aftershave.

'Is my sexual orientation important to you?' he said, some hope there in his voice.

'Indirectly. I would just like to know.'

'Yes, I am gay. And many people find that reassuring at a time like this. I should just go through the categories of charges.' Bill Golden smiled and pointed his gold fountain pen at the sheet. His sleeve rode up to reveal stiff white cuffs and gold links. 'There is the funeral home service charge, the merchandise charge.'

'Merchandise?'

'The casket, which we'll look at shortly.' He brought out a glossy brochure. At this point Jordan left the room. 'Or the urn.'

'Casket. That's what Susan wanted. To be buried.'

I remembered a conversation we had one night in

England, after the Virginia Woolf interlude. I was drunk, she was sober. We were exchanging funeral preferences because she said she was afraid she'd die in childbirth. I knew her well enough by then to try and talk her through it rather than out of it. Susan had a fear of being burned alive, she wanted a short Anglican service, she wanted me to say something about her life and after the service she wanted Joni Mitchell singing 'Amelia'. I said I had a fear of being buried alive so my preference was cremation. I wanted her to say something about my life and I wanted two songs: Otis Redding singing 'Try a Little Tenderness' and something else which I changed each day for the rest of the holiday. She said I was sentimental and just wanted to make people cry, whereas 'Amelia' had a significance all of its own. I said 'Try a Little Tenderness' always seemed to be a song about her so she accepted it.

Bill Golden smiled. 'I can't tell you how important that is. To know the deceased's wishes . . .'

'Yes. I'm sure it is.'

'There are incidental charges along the way which we'll pick up and bill you for subsequent to the burial: the notice in the newspapers, certain honorariums, etc. Other charges which we'll itemise: funeral stationery, I don't know whether you're considering a memorial guest register, but I would strongly recommend thank you cards which we'll administer and send to those who have kindly sent flowers. And on top of that, there will of course be a seven per cent goods and services tax. Even in death we are not exempt.'

They all came to the funeral but Angel stood out as we gathered at the grave. His grief was prouder; bigger; more magnificent. It was also more public, but then he was paying for the show.

Grief forces most of us into a dark corner of our own world: a private garden of tear-filled lakes and infinite emerald lawns, and an open grave which has been measured and cut and dug for us. For a while after Susan's death I climbed down into that place and lay there. Now and then we all find excuses to try our plot for size and some of us get comfortable in there and never climb out. I can tell you now that the earth is warm down there and the worms burrow through to find you and you don't feel claustrophobic, just a slow assimilation with the soil. I know I understood all this then, I'm not sure whether I understand it now.

I took Angel's advice. You can learn about people by observing them in their grief. Susan's father laid his arm on Jordan's shoulder and they both made their way to their own private place where they spent a few days together: just the two of them, the biological mourners. Jordan pasted metaphorical pictures onto the mausoleum walls and remembered holidays and bath-times and Susan's father did the same, each using the other as a surrogate for the woman who had deserted them. I led the spiritual mourners. Angel cried a whole soliloquy of pain. Chester stood proudly in a beautiful fawn suit and an immaculate white T-shirt, straight-backed; looking into the distance unblinking like a bugler playing the Last Post. Michael and Rosa linked their arms and tried to be strong for me, but they couldn't hold their bright, forced smiles and each time I turned away they collapsed onto each other and cried. Angela took some remedies and tried to force them on me – arnica and something else and I told her I didn't want them. She said she and some other women were holding a wake that evening. Even in death Angela was fighting to get Susan back. Carl doodayed through it, not even bothering to pretend an emotion he wasn't feeling. He murmured something about Kahlil Gibran and pushed a photocopied page of Carlos Castaneda into my hands. I told him I had no time for his chemical theism. He said that was cool, and high-fived it away, tugging off his ineptly tied necktie. He was not wearing shorts but had found a pair of crumpled chinos for the occasion. The girl from the agency desk came too. The one who I liked. I found myself standing next to her even though we were almost strangers. She said she came because her parents had brought her up to do these things but also because Chester had called her and told her. The rest, a few shabby artists and immaculate dealers, an albino jazz singer shading his eyes from the sun, some of Susan's school friends from Bellflower dressed in their Sunday church faces, filled the spaces in between. And that was how the day was spent. Apartment, chapel, graveside, apartment connected by sedate limousine rides, silent except for the mush and bump of wide tyres on affluent streets. The cortege provoked the stares of passers-by as they contemplated their own destiny in the hearse's mirrored glass. The day was a slow release of tension and a gradual build up of grief, no rituals to hold it at bay any longer, no arrangements to obsess away the pain.

The next morning Ray called me and asked me to come down to the station house. When I got there he showed me a report from the river police. The night before, a police launch had spotted a small blaze on the East River. They had gone to investigate and found four men standing in a small boat conducting some kind of ritual. The fire was an African fertility mask they had set light to before dropping it into the river. One of the men was Angel.

'What do you make of that?' Ray said, watching my face.

'I don't know.'

'I'll go talk to him.'

Ray also said that they had been questioning the superintendent at the apartment and there were a number of things he needed to check with me. He led the way from the cluttered communal central area into a side office, closed the half-glass door, waved me to a chair and threw a file onto the table.

He said, 'We've canvassed the area and now we have descriptions of all the men – as far as we can tell – who came out of your apartment block that night.' He picked up a sheet of paper and scanned it, then sat side on to the table. 'We're currently paying special attention to those the super either did not recognise or who he said visited irregularly.'

'Right.'

'Can I get you a coffee?'

'No.'

'Diet Coke?'

'No.'

'You OK with this?'

'Go on.'

'We showed the super some photographs – people who are known to us – but he didn't tie any of them up. The man said there was one guy left in a hurry. The super was watching TV but he had to come out to the hall to collect a package for one of the tenants. Mean anything to you?' He dipped again to his sheet. 'Early thirties, white, five ten/eleven, medium build, nice clothes, Ivy Leaguer, and with his head shaved? . . . John, does that mean anything to you?'

'No. It doesn't.'

15. In the Metal Forest

WE ALL JUMP to conclusions. Some conclusions are there to be jumped to. Like a bank on the other side of a narrow stream, you just have to do it. Police procedure, however, dictates that no conclusion should be drawn unless all indications to the contrary have been examined and dismissed. This makes the final conclusion the correct one because a tried and tested methodology has been employed. Ray did not assume that the bullet buried in the base of our bed had been fired from the .40 gun in our bedroom until it had been proven. A gizmo the New York Police Department use called IBIS – the 'Integrated Ballistic Identification System' – gave him the proof he needed. The gun was a new model – a Kahr K40 – which Susan had bought just a month before. The man in the shop had recommended it to her (his T-shirt said 'Happiness is a Warm Gun'). He said it was a DAO, which meant that there was little likelihood of the gun going off accidentally. The ammunition he sold her was Federal HiShock. Jordan wanted to see Susan's new gun so she let him hold it. Then she said he must never touch it again and he reluctantly agreed.

The accumulation of a huge number of such pieces of information (make of gun, type of cartridge, time of death, etc.) comprises what people in the law and order industry call the burden of proof. Proof is both a heavy and a fragile burden. You can drop it before you get a chance to deliver it to the right person. Your load may be contaminated by supposition and that is what the defence team is looking for. Supposition can taint the whole load. But if the burden is tended and nurtured and borne along by people like Ray it finally lands square in the lap of the person it belongs to: the perpetrator. And the perpetrator goes to prison for a long time. When Ray described the medium-built man with the bald head I tried to process the information in the way I already knew Ray would have done. I could find a thousand reasons for it not being Michael Conway and maybe two or three in support.

SoHo lies in late in the mornings, but not as late as Greenwich Village which rarely shows its face until after midday. As I walked away from the station, the sidewalk café tables were being wiped by waitresses in civilian clothing. Day workers congregated at the doorways of low-rise offices smoking the second lite cigarette of the morning and wishing they hadn't left their sunglasses in the office: coffee cups on the steps, lined and steaming like tiny chimneys. At the agency, Michael would be going to the washroom to move his bowels. In a small office you get to know people's habits. I decided to go and see him so I set off in that direction. Ten seconds later I changed my mind and headed back towards the hotel. Half a street later I turned into a bar. I couldn't face Jordan and Susan's father playing cards together or drawing aeroplanes on nice paper, or cooking some complex and ritualised meal that they didn't want to have to explain to me and I didn't want to know about. I just needed some temporary oblivion.

In the bar I ordered a Scotch and examined the reasons why it could have been Michael.

1. *He had never forgiven me and Susan for witnessing the puke episode.*

Unlikely, unless Michael, unbeknown to me, had started seeing Susan after we met up with him and Rosa that evening. Given a little more thought, this scenario seemed the most likely. In late January Rosa and Michael came to stay in our apartment. They needed a weekend away from the kids and some time alone together in the city so we let them have the spare room. The idea was that we wouldn't see much of them. In the event we stayed up late each night waiting for them to return from whichever show they'd been to and, when they got back, we talked. Rosa and I found a shared passion for alcohol and deep, profoundly unprofound soul searching, and Michael and Susan sipped water and flirted elegantly on the sofa and talked about Ron B. Kitaj, Jim Dine, David Hockney and any number of other artists I'd never heard of. The more they talked, the more it seemed they had in common. They had both been to the same exhibitions, they had both been students at the time of the mid 70s Pop Art in England Exhibition, and they had both seen it – Susan in Munich, Michael in Hamburg. And on and on. And by the end of the third evening there was a moment just before we all turned in when I kissed Rosa a little too long, and when I looked round Michael and Susan weren't there. Rosa wanted to cling on and take it further, but I wanted to find Susan and Michael so, giggling, we tiptoed through the apartment. Nothing. We looked in the bed-rooms. Nothing. Then I suddenly knew where they were and I wanted to go and find them on my own. In a way, this realisation was more painful than discovering them in bed together.

And there they were. On the roof, in the metal forest of TV and radio aerials, leaning on the railings and looking at the sky. Not touching or anything, just whispering, pointing, sharing some thoughts. I coughed; Susan turned round and, shamefaced, Michael would not meet my eye. He trooped back down to bed and Susan tried to keep me up there and point out to me what she had shared with Michael. Her heart wasn't really in it. She rarely took the trouble to hide what she was feeling from me. Sometimes she did with Jordan but Jordan could see through her. He was the only one who seemed capable of making her feel ashamed.

Michael and Rosa were gone by the time we got up the following day. They left a nice note and a bunch of flowers. We heard their whispered argument through the wall at 3 a.m. Most of it was from Michael who was pissed off at me for ogling Rosa. Anger displacing guilt. We just caught a few bitter words here and there: 'like that with me . . . kids . . . not easy . . . make time for you . . . work at it . . . sharing interests . . . feel that way about each other . . .'

2. *Michael had never forgiven me for making him shave his head.* However unlikely this seems as a motive, Michael Conway is a hugely vain man and it is, without stretching things too far, a distant possibility that vanity led him to first rape, then shoot Susan. I overstate the rape scenario. There is no evidence of a struggle. Nothing, as Ray cautiously told me, he'd expect to find. So just vanity. Maybe.

3. *Some other motive.* Adopting Ray's methodology I cannot dismiss some other motive that Michael may have had which I have no idea of. That's all.

The bar had no discernible name. It was not a theme bar. It was dark, sticky, and had no pretensions of being anything beyond what it was: the most efficient conduit between bottle and mouth. You stepped down into it off the street and ducked your head even though you didn't need to. The only light was blue neon. I sat on a stool. Each time I emptied my glass the barman filled it. Occasionally he'd give me a new one. From time to time he pushed a plate of salted nuts at me. The hours went on and on. CNN circulated the same stories on the hour every hour. I watched *Larry King Live* and numerous adverts for numerous homegrown hotel chains. The message was clear – you can stay in a little bit of America wherever you travel in the world. To enhance this message the news in between the ads illustrated just how dangerous the rest of the world could be. A woman in a flak jacket stood in front of a bullet-pitted building. Each time they showed the report she ducked at the same point. Dust kicked up behind her as a mortar thudded in. Something had happened in Northern Ireland. The Prime Minister stood gravely at a lectern voicing the same sound bite. El Niño had wreaked its havoc on another coastline. The same woman cried and pointed towards a crumpled shack. A new famine was advertised by a shot of matchstick children with swollen bellies swatting flies from their weeping eyelids on a heat-soaked plain. New news came and superseded old. Old news became round-ups. (Round-ups become Archive. Archive becomes Review of the Year. Review of the Year becomes history.) Every so often the barman (a college graduate working through the summer before embarking on a year of world travel) surfed through the local channels and fledgling or former CNN anchors switched their expressions to match the tone of their stories: serious for hard news, empathetic for tragedy, jaunty for politics and the money report and a twinkle for the octogenarian double marriage and the handover to the weather person. The student barman was growing a beard but it wasn't taking. It looked like the kind of beards some Mexicans have – as though they haven't shaved for three days but still intend to get round to doing so, whereas the jaw hair is actually the result of three weeks' concerted endeavour.

On the 7 p.m. local news, under the caption 'Manhattan

Shooting', the exterior of the agency flashed up behind a newsman. I called for the college boy to turn up the sound. Panicked, he changed channels, then he changed back and the sound came up; '. . . Conway arrested earlier today in connection with the shooting of art dealer, Susan Wayne.' We saw Michael being led blinking out of the building by Ray and another detective. They slowed so Ray could smile at the newsman, then Michael was pushed into the back of a blue-and-white police car and driven away. Jake Friend handed back to the studio and we were promised regular updates.

I found a phone and called the hotel. Jordan answered. He sounded scared. He asked where I had been because he was frightened that I'd been shot too. I heard Susan's father ask him something and he told him it was Dad, calling from a bar somewhere. I told Jordan I was sorry and that I was coming home and that I promised I'd read him a story if he wanted. He said he hadn't had a story read to him in six years but could I bring him some Coke. I said I would and rang off before I had to speak to the old man. Then I called Ray. It took them a few minutes to find him. I heard somebody laughing in the main office, another man telling a detailed joke, not a practised joke-teller so he was being careful he got it right. The TV played in the background, somebody whistling, a woman calling goodnight, then the phone was picked up.

'Where have you been?' Ray said.

'In a bar.'

'You saw the news?'

'Yes.'

'So you know we arrested Conway?'

'Yes.'

'I'm sure you have your reasons,' Ray said, 'but don't try and get involved in the process, Mr Wayne. And if myself or another detective asks you questions to which you know the answers, please be good enough to supply them . . . Do you know what I'm saying?'

'Yes.'

'Goodnight.'

I walked back to the hotel feeling like I'd lost a good friend. Then I stopped at a pay phone and asked for Ray again.

I said, 'Ray. I'm sorry.'

He said he was sorry too and it had been a long day and he knew what I'd been going through. We said goodnight again but this time with the argument healed and Ray asking me to come down to see him tomorrow morning. When I got back to the hotel I diverted into the bar for one last drink. Back in the room, Susan's father was asleep on my bed. I went in to see Jordan. He was lying on his bed in his pyjamas, awake, staring at the ceiling. I sat down on the bed.

'I'm sorry,' I said, and tried to stroke his hair. He pulled away.

'You smell of drink and cigarettes. Did you get the Coke?'

'. . . I'll order some from room service.'

'They just have Pepsi.'

'I'll go out and get some for you.'

'I'm not thirsty.'

'. . . How's Gramps bearing up?'

'He keeps crying.'

I felt a lump in my throat. I had to turn away so Jordan wouldn't see me but something burst through and I lay down beside him and wept. Susan's father came to the door and saw me and looked disgusted. I got off the bed and pushed past him and went back downstairs to the bar. I talked at the people around me and cried through some more drinks. At 3 a.m. I went back up. Jordan and Gramps were asleep and

the room felt peaceful again. I threw up in the bathroom
then lay down on the couch and tried to sleep.

16. Me and Jordan go on a Trip – 2

JORDAN HAD HIS feet up on the dash, he was reading from a booklet the park ranger had handed us when we stopped and asked directions to the Grant Village Camp: 'Food, garbage, and any odorous – what's odorous?'

'Smelly.'

'. . . items used for preparing and/or eating food must be properly stored whenever they are not being carried or used. Day or night.'

We'd been travelling together for a week and a half. Eight days since we left Cody. The van smelt like ours now. We'd moved on from the initial silence to a kind of buddyish bonhomie. Jordan in fact would not stop talking and it had got to the point where I was beginning to crave some peace and quiet. Yellowstone Park was projecting itself onto the windshield of the camper van. Too big to be real, too many mountains, too many pine trees.

'Do not approach wildlife. Feeding, disturbing or harassing wildlife is prohibited. Yeah, like we're really going to harass a grizzly bear.' Jordan looked over at me. I nodded him on. 'Fires are allowed only in designated fire rings and must be attended at all times. How would you like a fire in your ring, Dad?'

'Ouch.'

We were booked in at the 'Grant Village Campgrounds'. This satisfied our two main criteria: that we be by water and that we be near bears. Grant Village is on the west tip of Yellowstone Lake. The woman on the phone told us it opened up in June when the bears had stopped feeding on the spawning fish and closed in October. The cost was sixteen dollars a night. We booked for a week.

'It says they have flush toilets, showers, firewood and a dump station. Why do they need to say that twice?'

'Say what twice?'

'Flush toilets and dump station. Like, what is the difference?'

'Oh, I see. A joke. Is that Yellowstone Lake?' To the left of us a plane of still silver-blue water was showing through a fringe of pines.

Jordan looked at the map. 'Did we come in from the south or the west entrance?'

'South.' A half-hour queue, then we were into the captive wilderness. Jordan said the gate was to stop the lakes and pines getting out and breeding and taking over the cities. He was reading a science fiction novel at the time.

'It's Lewis Lake.' Jordan put down the map and the rules and picked up his book, *Into the Dark Headfirst*. I was afraid I'd punctured his mood by not laughing at the joke so I said, 'Where is Herb now?'

'Orbiting Mars.'

Herb Todd is a water miner. The water on earth has run out and he's on a mission to save the world. He's nursed *Quom Bandit*, his beaten-up cargo freighter, to Mars, where he and babe scientist Lorna Golightly are intending to blast chunks out of the permafrost and then tow them back home in fantastic metal nets. What Lorna had not yet done was to work out how to stop the permafrost melting when they re-

115

entered the earth's atmosphere, but Jordan and I reckoned the chances were that she would. Herb hadn't screwed her yet, which is what I'd been waiting for. Jordan thought she'd turn out to be a robot.

'Have they started the blasting yet?'

'Soon. When Lorna's activated the charges. The ship is leaking some stuff into the oxygen and it's making them go all gooey together. Lorna can't keep her mind on her work.'

'Right.'

He bowed his head again. We passed a sign for Old Faithful and another to West Thumb and Grant. Soon the road split and we turned right into the campsite. Jordan fished out the piece of paper and read off the site number, C84. To his delight, it was close to the dump station. We parked. Jordan vaulted down and I climbed stiffly out. Next to us was a blue Ford Galaxy with Minnesota plates, beyond that another camper. The site on the left was empty. The next one down was a huge trailer van with a silver stove vent sticking out of the roof, fuming like a behemoth smoking a pipe. Tents in various primary colours were pitched close to the vans. The air was very clean. In the silence my ears reached for something industrial. All they came up with was a whining generator, a van engine coming slowly along the road towards the site, an outboard motor on the lake.

'So . . . ?' I said, kneading my back with my knuckles, pulling the damp shirt away from my spine.

'Cool,' Jordan said.

'Eat or walk?'

'Explore.'

We locked the van and trailed off towards the lake. The campsite was virtually uninhabited. In the next clearing a woman was hanging shirts on a makeshift line tied between a green Jeep Cherokee and a tree. Also suspended on it were three carrier bags of supplies. She took a wooden peg from her mouth, smiled at Jordan, then me, and said, 'Come far?'

'New York City,' I said.

'Wow.'

The woman was wearing brown canvas shorts, like Carl's. They had a different effect on me than Carl's did. She had a tight white vest on over tiny breasts, an open, outdoor face and long, long blonde hair. Jordan gave her the eye then started to walk on.

'You guys just arrived?'

'Yes. Just.'

'I'm Mary.' She pegged the tails of another small Timberland shirt onto the line.

'John,' I said, 'John Wayne.' I walked towards her holding out my hand. I wanted to touch her.

She laughed and shook my hand.

'Come on, Dad,' Jordan called from some way away.

'I have two girls around your son's age. A little younger. Your son, yes?' Mary said.

'Yes.'

No, I have not abducted him, Mary, no he is not my stepson, no he is not my nephew.

'I guess they'll be along and find him. Especially when I tell them you're from New York City. New faces, new games, right?'

'Dad. Come On!' Jordan was far, far away now.

'Later, then,' I said and walked on up the track towards the lake.

'Anything you need. Just ask,' Mary said. 'Ranger office that way. Shop that way.'

'Thanks.'

I found Jordan balancing one-legged on a log, his hands in his jeans pockets to maintain coolness, which made the task harder. He was looking out at the huge lake. I stood with him and marvelled for a while. Neither of us needed to say anything and, for once, Jordan didn't. We just took it in: the stillness, the flatness, the black fringe of the trees. Breathing it in like oxygen, eating it up like food. Jordan finally overbalanced and fell onto his knee which he grazed badly enough to warrant us going back to the camper, unpacking, pitching the tent and doing all the other housekeeping business you have to do when you go camping. By now we had a routine. I'd lay out the tarpaulin while Jordan undid the tent, set the pegs next to each other, and fetched the mallet. Then we'd put up the tent between us trying to beat our previous record of three minutes and fourteen seconds. Breathless we'd pop a can each (Budweiser and Coke), then Jordan would scout for firewood if we needed any and I'd make a start on cooking up some food which involved opening tins of tuna and boiling up pasta.

While we were eating, the owner of the Ford Galaxy showed. A weather-beaten old man with a fishing rod and flies tied round his cap, walking wearily, like he was dragging a sledge. He sighed a lot, made heavy weather of unlocking the back of the Galaxy and pulling out a maple rocking chair ('too heavy, why the Hell I brought this I'll never know'), lighting his fire ('wood round here's too wet'), opening up his can of stew ('don't make can openers like they used to'). Jordan and I shook our heads at each other as the Old Bastard, refusing all offers of food, help or beer, muttered his way through his routine. Just our luck when we could have pitched up next to Mary and her two.

'Do you want anything else?' I said, as Jordan laid his tin plate on the ground.

'No thanks.'

Old Bastard was grunting, 'Now where is that cas-sette tape I'm sure I left it on the seat this morning now where did I put that damned tape ah here it is here you are now let's just put it in the slot here and see what we have here just listen up to what we have here . . .'

I asked Jordan, 'What do you want to do?'

'Scout around?'

'I'll wash up. Your turn tomorrow.'

'Deal.'

'Don't go far. And watch for the grizzlies.'

'OK.'

'Back by ten.'

'OK.'

'Are you listening, Jordan?'

'OK.'

I watched him out of the clearing. Smaller and smaller until he was gone behind the trees. Old Bastard had his tape on now, a Viennese waltz compilation. He must have put it together himself because some of the pieces cut off before they finished, others started late. Old Bastard harrumphed along to the music, eating his hot stew, occasionally firing a question at me over the top of the Galaxy as I washed the plates. When I'd finished I tried to read some of Jordan's book.

Half an hour later Jordan ran up trailing two miniature versions of Mary the peg lady. He was excited, excitable, 'Dad, Dad, I need some money, just five dollars. Dad, Dad . . .'

'What for?' I handed him a ten.

'They have these really cool pens in the shop. I really need one.'

'Are you going to introduce me to your friends?'

'This is Samantha.' He half swung to his left. 'And this is Claudine.' He did the same to his right.

'Hello Samantha. Hello Claudine.'

They nodded and stood, frozen, for a second.

'Well shoot off, then.'

They turned and ran, laughing away. Old Bastard muttered something about 'peace and quiet come here to get away from kids piss through your letter box, put shit in your mail box . . .'

At that moment if Jordan had asked me for a thousand dollars, I'd have given it to him. Anything was worth it to see him smile. To hear him laugh like a child again. I dropped off to sleep on my cot just before Lorna Golightly pressed the button to arm the charges.

Old Bastard woke in the night. I heard him cry out. Jordan didn't stir. Then I heard a wolf and a dog started barking. All that life there outside the tent just waiting.

I walked up to the boat launch and stared out. A man was fishing far out, probably asleep. I watched the boat drift for a while then carried on along the track, over the small bridge, and up the trail towards the amphitheatre. What I was looking for didn't seem to be there so I headed back to the camp. I looked along the line towards Mary and the girls' tent, hoping that by some fluke she couldn't sleep either and was sitting up smoking some grass or drinking beer. She wasn't.

Who we are is where we are and who we're with. Being with Jordan was good, being in that huge beautiful space was good. Being with myself felt old and worn out; looking to Carol to help me and knowing I'd chosen her because she wasn't free to; looking towards Angel for advice and guidance and knowing he was deeply flawed so I couldn't trust much of what he said. So all that was left was Susan, and Susan was only there in the silences, when I trusted myself with my sober company and I listened to her and she told me what to do. And on those occasions, like then, by the lake, on the way back to Jordan, what she said was, 'Help Jordan because, in his own way, Jordan is reaching out to you for your help.'

★

Next morning Samantha and Claudine came ragging at the flap of the tent before Jordan or I were awake. When we'd unzipped they fell over each other to make the offer. They said their mom said do you want to come and have some breakfast with us, and we should come soon because it will get cold and not to bring anything, just our appetites. One more look at each other to check they hadn't missed anything out and two brown, dungareed girls dervished out of the clearing. Old Bastard popped his grizzled head out of his flap, looked up to see whether he should moan about the rain, and because he couldn't, looked over and called, 'Another hot one', as if this was the very last thing people camping out in the open wanted. An animal of some description had laid a huge turd next to his tent. Jordan spotted it and laughed.

As we were walking to Mary's, Jordan's hair flattened down with cold water, last clean T-shirt on, me in best Levis and rollneck, we debated whether some people give off special pheromones. What these do is make people want to piss or shit all over them. Jordan, of course, stuck with the literal and chortled. I spun it into the metaphorical and he lost the thread of what I was trying to say. By the time we'd reached Mary's we were in knots. Metaphorically.

Mary was bright-eyed and freshly washed. She was cooking bacon and eggs, tomatoes and mushrooms. There was a plate of warm bread on the table, some frankfurters bubbling in a tin pot over a small fire, and a pot of coffee. On the trestle table, serviettes which we were told the girls had folded for us. So we applauded the folding and everybody became very bright and talkative and the breakfast was laughter and questions and history and hopes and more laughter. Not even a stumble when Claudine finally plucked up her courage to ask Jordan what she'd been wanting to know since she met him – where his mom was – and Jordan sailed through it saying, 'Oh, she died', in such a way as to keep the burdensome cloud of reality away from us and anchored far out over the lake. Mary caught the harmonic of pain and winced. She looked at me with a 'We'll come back to this later' look, then she loaded some more bacon onto Jordan's plate. It was his party now. The girls, one on each side of him, tussled for his attention, Mary mothered him, and I, proudly, sat sharing him with people who didn't know about the rest of it.

The wave of our enthusiasm carried us through the pot-washing, built as the girls threw water around and wasn't even diminished when Mary had to take Samantha not quite out of earshot for some serious talk about her always taking things too far. All she'd done was to wet Jordan's T-shirt, but Jordan made the mistake of saying it was his last clean one and Mary took this on board as Jordan missing his mom. She didn't actually vocalise this, but she knew and I knew that's what she felt. Samantha came back and apologised and Jordan, good boy that he can be sometimes, threw water over her. So he was the bad one, except he couldn't be because his mom, etc.

It was decided that as we'd started the day together, we should see the day out together. And as neither of our parties had been to see Old Faithful, we climbed into Mary's jeep and drove out to West Thumb, then on to the geyser. We parked up behind the reception and the kids spilled out and away. A millisecond later they were back saying there was a clock which told you when the thing was going to go off next and we had half an hour to wait. Mary took charge of issuing the orders about not wandering too far away and I got talking to one of the guides. She had a bright, retiree's enthusiasm for trivia.

'The early travellers out here messed up some of the geysers by washing their clothes in them.'

'That so?'

'And Old Faithful doesn't spout like it used to.'

More people wandered up. Free information: as good as it gets.

'We have most of the world's major geysers here or hereabouts,' she told us as if she'd personally travelled the world and rounded them up. We nodded. 'All within a few miles of Old Faithful.'

'OK?' Mary wandered up.

'Hi.'

She made a move to take my arm, then pulled away at the last moment. 'I'm sorry,' she said. 'I . . .'

'Walk?'

'Yes.'

We moved away from the crowds. Because Mary had made a mess of the arm thing we couldn't touch. It had become an issue, whereas it wasn't before. Now we were alone, without the kids to talk through, she was coy, I was embarrassed. We had nothing to say. I knew she wanted to ask about Susan but conversations like that are for the end of a day, a few bottles of beer down the line, so I asked about her.

'Well . . .' she crossed her arms. 'I was married. But I'm not now.'

'. . . OK.'

'And . . . and he doesn't know where we are. The girls do not know this.'

'Go on.'

We moved further away from the gift shop and the expectant campers, and the line of four-wheel-drives arriving and disgorging more geyser watchers.

'See, he was violent. Towards me.'

'I'm sorry,' was all I could think of to say.

She pushed on quickly, 'But not towards the girls.' She

stopped, faced me, and lifted up her hair from her forehead. It hid a long scar which followed her hairline. She lifted her vest and showed me a scar on her midriff. 'There are more, but I don't know you well enough yet.' Then she was shy again and laughed, pretending she hadn't meant to imply anything. I saw three children watching us, waiting to see how we got on.

What I wanted to say was that I was not a violent man. That, while I could take no responsibility for the action of her husband, I felt I had to apologise for it on behalf of all the other men I knew. But what I felt, when I saw the scar on her stomach, was revulsion. Susan's body had been violated too, but Susan's scars never healed. We walked back to the crowds in silence, the kids fell into step behind us, picking up our muted mood.

Old Faithful ejaculated massively into the air and kept coming and coming. I expected it all to be over but it went on for five minutes. After the initial shock, the cries and whoops from the crowd, everybody got itchy feet. We'd seen it, now we wanted to go and see something else. Afterwards the kids went on some postcoital spending in the gift shop and I went to sit in the jeep. Mary diplomatically stayed outside, saying she had to watch the kids.

We drove straight back to camp and split. It was midday and we all pretended we hadn't made arrangements beyond lunch. Jordan thanked the girls for breakfast. I thanked Mary and we walked away; I tried to strike up a lively conversation with Jordan which would carry back to the girls, just to prove there was no ill-feeling, but Jordan wouldn't bite, because he knew there was. He lay on his cot all afternoon, reading his book, and I sat outside and drank down half a bottle of Scotch. I had just one left. Old Bastard turned up at dusk, said hello, turned on his tape, and cooked a fish he'd caught. He didn't offer to share. I ignored his questions and eventually he stopped asking them. Jordan and I ate in silence. Once, for a second or so, he forgot he was mad at me and asked whether we should cook breakfast for the girls tomorrow. When I said that wasn't a good idea he remembered and clammed up again. After the meal he asked whether he could go and see the girls again. I said he could but not to be back too late.

I drank the Scotch and watched the sun set. Then, in the clearing, I saw Mary. I didn't know how long she'd been there, but she was watching me. She was wearing a long cardigan, jeans, not shorts. Her arms were crossed over her chest. I waved her to come and sit with me because this is what she seemed to want me to do. She walked slowly towards me. Old Bastard grunted a greeting and Mary managed a smile. She sat on the damp ground beside me. I offered her the canvas chair and she declined it so I fetched a rug from the van, found another glass and we shook out the rug and sat cross-legged together. Some preamble later – the kids, the day, the geyser, more thanks for the breakfast – she apologised before I had the chance to.

'No, my fault. My fault entirely,' I said, staring away into the black of the trees.

I heard, 'I do this. I give too much too soon.'

'You felt it was right. Don't blame yourself for that. Blame me.'

'I don't want to blame anybody. I'd just like us to have another chance.' Too frank.

'So let's just enjoy each other's company,' I said. 'It doesn't get much better than this.' I smiled a cheesy smile at the sky, waved at the trees, held up my glass. We chinked and cheered. She put down her glass and moved a little closer.

'More?' I held up my last bottle.

'No. I've had enough.'

'Right.' I put it down again.

'So, Jordan's mother. Your wife. Tell me what happened.'

'OK ... OK. But first ...' I stood up. 'I have to ...' I pointed towards the dump station. 'Mind the Scotch.' I stumbled away, buying time. I did not want to talk about Susan to Mary. I did not want to talk about anything to Mary. I wanted Mary and her scars and her over-ebullient kids to drive back to the abusive husband and leave me alone. I pissed Scotch. It came out treacly and yellow. My liver felt tired, as if it would give anything for a couple of litres of spring water. Tough shit. I zipped up and headed slowly back. I caught sight of Jordan and the two girls going into the shop, a ranger idly conversing with a new couple on the step. Mary was lying on the rug looking up at the stars, her cardigan was open and she was showing her white vest, nipples hard in the cold pointing up at the slice of phosphorescent moon. Old Bastard was walking around, pretending to be clearing up but taking the opportunity of looking at the pretty woman on the rug. I knelt beside her, hoping she'd sit up. She didn't. She patted the earth beside her, obliging me to lie.

'Look ...' I said, after racking my brains for something interesting or wistful to say about the stars.

'No,' Mary said. 'Don't talk.'

We lay there for a while in silence, not touching, then Mary said, 'Like I said. I give too much too soon.' She scrambled to her feet. 'Goodnight, John,' she said and walked away.

Old Bastard called something. It sounded like 'fool', but it could have been 'cruel', or it could have been one of his repertoire of vocal mannerisms signifying satiation, hunger, anger, indigestion or lust. I lay for a while longer, wondering what time it was, whether I should get round to calling Carol and apologising for not having called for over a week, and finally thinking about Ray and what it was he wanted to tell me. Then, despite everything, I started wondering about Mary. How she would look naked. How her ass would feel in my hands. How her breath would taste, how her breasts would taste. Just drunken idiot longings that bypassed any kind of morality.

Mary was sitting inside the jeep listening to the weather on the radio. The white interior light washed all the colour from her face. When she saw me she launched a smile, turned off the radio, and climbed out. She closed the jeep door and leaned against it. I walked up to her, put my arms round her and kissed her. Her mouth was open and wet and wanting. Already she was breathing faster. I wondered how long it had been for her. How long since she and the abusive husband did it. Or perhaps they did it all the time but he needed to hit her to excite himself. I pulled away. Mary reached between us, down below our waists where our hips were still making contact, and touched me, all the time looking into my face.

'Is this what you want?' she said.

'Yes.'

'This?' She tried something different, then something different again. I was moving beyond speech. Then she pulled her hand away. 'Not tonight,' she said and watched to see how I reacted. I straightened up and swallowed.

'OK.'

'It's late,' she said, looking over towards the edge of the clearing. Nearly ten, and on cue, the girls ran towards us then slowed when they saw who their mother was with.

'Goodnight then.' I took Mary's hand, squeezed it, let it fall.

'Goodnight, John.' The girls walked to her and she held them, one under each arm.

I looked back when I reached the last vehicle. They were still standing together, watching me. From that distance it looked like the girls were protecting their mother, not the other way round.

Next morning Jordan went round to see if the girls wanted to come out on the lake with us. We'd decided to hire a boat for the day. Three or four minutes later he came back and told me that they'd gone. The man in the next pitch said he heard them leave in the night.

'I'm sorry,' I said to my son.

'Sure.' Jordan slunk back into the tent and lay on his cot for the rest of the day.

17. Panic and Phobias

THE MORNING AFTER Michael Conway was arrested I went to see Ray. The office looked like it hadn't been painted for twenty years. The air-conditioning units anchored on alternate windows clattered and cooled the air to an uncomfortable degree. All the phones seemed to be ringing. When the civilian administrative assistants answered them they shouted names across the fields of desks. A young woman was marched through by another woman holding her by the leopard-skin sleeve and collar of her cat-suit. Ray came out of a side room. He was detained on his way across to me by a man in a good suit who suavely exuded authority. They exchanged a few words, Ray moved off, the man called something, Ray shrugged and deferred. The man walked into an office, pulling the door shut behind him. I smelt strong perfume, looked round and a woman was leaning down and handing me a cup of coffee. I took it. Ray sat on the desk. He looked tired: red-eyed.

'Is Michael here?' I said.

'Yeah.' Ray looked like he was waiting for another apology to add to the one from the night before. I offered one but he shrugged it off.

'How is he?'

'Looking good for a homicide. How should he be?'

'What happens now?' I said, uncomfortable with the weight of scrutiny I was bearing.

'He talks to his lawyer when he's a little calmer. He makes the decision whether he wants to call a bailbondsman. He says nothing on the advice of his lawyer who sits in and advises and we're playing this game for a while and finally . . .' Ray chewed his thumbnail. 'Let's get out of here.'

He fetched his jacket from a room of vented metal lockers. A man was in there changing into shorts and running shoes. The room smelt of fresh sweat. I followed Ray downstairs as he pulled his blue linen jacket round him. Outside he turned left and walked fast, I tried to keep pace with him but he didn't seem to want me to so I fell back and he slackened his speed but kept two steps ahead. On the next corner he turned into a coffee bar and we were back into the Siberian blast of another air-conditioned interior. Ray called for two espressos over the heads of the people three deep at the counter. The pretty waitress broke the surface of her day and smiled her favoured-customer greeting. Ray sat down at a table by the door and slung his jacket over the back of the seat. I faced him and waited.

He said, 'You know what I'm thinking?'

'. . . No.'

'I can't read you.' For a moment I thought he was going to arrest me. 'I can't read you. I'm thinking I have you all worked out. I'm wrong.'

'Why do you feel you need to work me out?'

'Do you know what I'm saying?'

I shrugged.

He said, 'You don't want to tell me I've got it wrong?' He tugged up his sleeves, unbuttoning his cuffs, getting ready to do business.

'I don't know what you're talking about.'

'I have to ask you a question . . . Do you believe Michael Conway killed your wife?'

'Surely the question is whether you believe Michael Conway killed my wife.'

'I'm asking you.' Ray picked a toothpick out of a small glass pot, leaned back in his seat and pricked at his front teeth with it. 'This is what I can't square. What I can't square is why John Wayne goes to a bar for twelve hours the day after his wife is murdered, fails to make contact with either the police or his son, then he's surprised when I suggest he's acting out of character.'

'That's what you mean is it, about not reading me?'

'Yeah.'

'You've known me for forty-eight hours, Ray. How can you possibly judge what is and what is not in character?'

'That's what they pay me to do. I thought I had. That's all I'm saying.' He held out his hands, palms up. 'I don't like surprises.'

'And what . . . ?'

'So is there something I should know?'

'About what?'

'I don't know. You want to tell me?'

'Have you been speaking to Angela?'

'I've been talking to a lot of people.'

'And what is your point exactly?'

'I don't have a point.' Ray looked lazily over at the counter.

'Tell me about Michael.'

'Michael?'

'Yes.'

'Not "Conway" – or "that slimebucket"? Just Michael?'

'Yes.'

At this point, Ray relinquished control of the conversation. He'd said what he came to say and now he relaxed.

'OK. Sometimes it happens when a man like Conway gets caught, thinking he's got his whole life worked out; money, success, children, wife, nice house in a nice neighbourhood. That's a lot to trade in for a period of time behind bars with people who might not appreciate the finer things of life. Might not appreciate what his upbringing has given him. More than that, might decide he owes them something in return. All of this goes through his mind. So he starts climbing the walls, screaming to be let out.'

The waitress brought the coffees over, leaning down to give Ray a look down her cleavage. Her big white breasts were hammocked in black lace, between them a triangle of darkness. Ray didn't go for it. She walked away, disappointed. Ray stirred three sugars into the tiny cup. Two stirs clockwise, two anti-clockwise, two clockwise, then he tapped the spoon on the silver rim of the tiny white cup and laid it in the saucer.

I said, 'Can I see him?'

'No.'

'You're angry that I disappeared yesterday?'

'Not angry. Confused.' His head was angled towards the table, he was paying considerable attention to the grains of sugar that had been spilt on it.

'People don't visit bars after they find their spouses murdered?'

'Some do. There are no rules. Except that, however people decide to deal with whatever it is they're feeling, they usually stay in touch because a large part of what they are feeling early on is curiosity. Human nature. They're curious to discover who has deprived them of their partner. Those that loved their spouses, those that hated their spouses, no difference. Curiosity. Curiosity about the why, the how, the who. You have curiosity about the how and the why. You don't exhibit curiosity about the who. Which leads me towards my confusion.'

'You're saying I already knew Michael killed her?'

He lifted his head. 'Did you?'

'No.'

'Did you suspect?'

'No.'

'Does this fact surprise you?'

'It fits.'

'Did you collude with Michael Conway?'

'Should you be reading me my rights for this conversation?'

'You tell me.'

Ray didn't believe that. Not for a moment. He was tired. I'd disappointed him. Ray thought he had the world worked out and then he came across an Englishman called John Wayne who didn't conform. I don't know how Ray had it worked out so I don't know what he expected me to be. Perhaps shock has recognisable stages which I didn't exhibit. Perhaps I was supposed to feel guilty. Perhaps I was supposed to be angry, or in denial, or in some other textbook psychological state. What I felt at that point about Michael was not anger. I knew I should have felt this and if I tried hard enough I could even conjure some up but I have always had difficulty equating my emotions with what I see other people exhibiting.

If this was a film there would now be an expositional moment in which John Wayne would be portrayed by a child actor. The scene would be grainy or in black and white and the child (bearing only a distant resemblance to our hero) would walk in on his mother screwing a stranger, or find his father dead from a self-inflicted gunshot wound to his temple, or be standing in front of an uncle who would be caressing him inappropriately. Some backstory sufficiently mordant to explain the character flaw to the audience and to render it harmless. A begets B so if you haven't suffered A you won't suffer from B. When I was a child I hit an older boy over the head with a toy pistol. Does that count? When I was a child, for much of the time, I wore hand-me-down clothes that didn't fit. How about that? When I was a child I was loved as well as I could be by my mother. Who was ever scarred by somebody doing their best in difficult circumstances?

My psychoanalyst said I protested too much. She said I should examine the proposition that my denigration of my past was part of my low self-esteem: I downgrade the abuse because I undervalue myself. By then I'd had six months of Cyn-the-shrink: more than enough. I screamed at her about how people in her profession use abuse as a catch-all term just to make things seem worse than they actually are. Abuse is to the psychoanalysis industry what fire is to the fire department. I said there is no way I suffered abuse in my childhood. No way. She said, 'Why does the assertion make you so angry?' Sweat glistened on her moustache.

I said, 'No, you don't get me like that.'

'*Get* you?'

'Don't play that game with me, Cynthia.'

'All right . . . so why do you use the fire analogy?'

Cynthia shared the floor with a beefy acupuncturist, a pranic healer, a colour therapist and a pretty Japanese bulimic (beautifully defined delicate features like a line drawing) who sold detoxification diets and vitamin therapy. She was the compulsive handwasher who was always locked in the toilet when you needed to go.

'It just came out. It doesn't signify anything. No, don't smile, Cynthia. It doesn't.'

I walked out. When I got home I wrote to her. I had to finish what I was trying to say.

Dear Cynthia,

What your smile prevented me from saying was just how wrong you are about me. How can you be so wrong? I know that you feel your part of the bargain is to bring to my attention my verbal tics so I can examine them and, in so doing, presumably, gain some insight into my 'condition'. The truth is that I chose fire because originally I was going to use crime and the police department as an analogy. Then I realised that if I did you'd make the assumption that abuse was the crime perpetrated against me. So I chose fire instead. OK, so you picked up on that. It wasn't so clever. I know myself better than you think I do. Yes, I can already see you nodding and asking me to define 'know'. This is what you've done to me. You've made me question everything about myself. I can no longer have a conversation with anybody without examining it from every angle. Soon I will no longer be capable of breathing without thinking the breaths in and out. When I fall asleep I shall die. You will be responsible. You swore you'd help me, Cynthia. When I came to you and you asked what I wanted, do you remember what I said? I said I want parole: I want to be released from the sentence of being me. I laughed. You didn't. And so we wasted four or five sessions back and forth about jailers and who holds the key and what the sentence is for, on and on. You said it would get easier. Why is it no easier? Another thing. Language is nothing. Language is too far down the chain to mean anything. By the time anything gets said it has been processed so many times that the meaning has become redundant. So we skirt round each other's islands, playing in the sand. If you want to join Kurtz on that river journey to the Heart of Darkness you won't do it by talking, Cynthia. Don't you know that? OK, it's exhausting being me. Did you prompt me to say that or did I just offer it? But I have no choice. I came to you for a choice. I hate you for not providing me with a choice, Cynthia. I hate the perfume you wear. I hate that you're a member of a sex I largely admire. I hate your moustache. Another thing: I was going to say arsonists. What arsonists are to the fire department. Then you'd have felt obliged to say something about abusers being the arsonists and abuse/fire is the result. Or maybe I would. Maybe I did. At least I did in my head. See. It's easy. I can do it. If I can do it, why don't more people do it? Another thing. Why did you not answer my questions about your sex life? Saying that you were intrigued to know why I needed to know is not an answer. I do know about you. I know all about you. I know why you chose those shitty books for your shelves and why you move them round each week so it looks like you've been reading them. And it's not so subtle when you transpose two of them. For example, three weeks ago you swapped *Panic and Phobias Vol. 2* (Berlin: Springer Verlag – I looked) with your unread 1948 edition of *Grays Anatomy*. If you ever tried to open that book it would fall apart in your hands. Try it. The slab of *American Psychologist* has solidified. *Social Skills and Mental Health* has been missing for a month. (Did the bulimic borrow it? – If so, it didn't work.) And treat Lazarus and Abramovitz on emotive imagery with caution. Their theories remain unexamined in a controlled environment. I promise I'll let you have it back when I've finished it. Incidentally, if the Japanese handwasher comes to you for help I think I've identified her problem. Try her out on Taijin-Kyofu-Sho. Know what that is? It's a Japanese syndrome characterised by fear of other people. TKS patients are afraid that their behaviour will embarrass or offend other people. It's very common in Japan and Prince and Tcheng-Laroche (1987) argue that it may constitute a culture-bound syndrome.

Get her to call me, I've done some research for her. I know exactly why you chose that chintz cloth (and I could take a stab at where you bought it). I know what to say to make your hand move towards the panic button. I even know what kind of session the woman before me has had. No, I don't listen. I look in the wastepaper basket and see how many tissues are in there. Are you messing her head up as well, Cynthia? No, you cannot be my mother. Why did you feel you had to ask? Yes, you did ask. Don't you know that everything in your room screams out that request. No wedding ring, Cynthia. Sweat on the moustache, Cynthia. Faint musty menopausal smell, Cynthia. No, the cheap perfume does not mask it. No, you cannot be my mother, the position has already been taken. I came to you for answers, Cynthia, and all you offered me were more questions. Sometimes there are easy answers. Sometimes you don't have to ask and ask and get deeper and deeper to find the right answer. Sometimes it's staring you in the face. But then your profession needs questions like the Criminal Courts need the law. You figure it out. OK, it's about the language of prosecution and how we convict ourselves each time we open our mouths. Please stop bothering me. Get out of my life and get one of your own. Cynthia.

A couple of months after Susan's death I thought I might go back and see Cynthia. Just to fill her in on things, but I decided against it. Each day that has passed since I walked out on her has felt like a small victory. The longer I stay away the bigger the victory. Let her wonder what I'm feeling and how I am. I know she does.

Back at the café, I was asking, 'Is there something you want me to say, Ray? Some way in which I can help you?'

'Your son,' Ray said. 'How's he taking it?'

'Bearing up.'

'So what does "bearing up" mean? Is this an English term?'

'It means he's not lying on the floor crying his eyes out.'

'Bearing up?'

'Yes.'

'And you consider this to be a good thing?'

'It's how he's choosing to deal with it.'

'Why aren't you with him now?'

'He's with his grandfather.'

'This is the father of your wife?'

'That's right.'

'How's he feel about Michael Conway?'

'I don't know.'

'You haven't asked him?'

'We haven't spoken.'

'About Conway?'

'No. We haven't spoken.'

Ray endeavoured to take this in.

'Susan's father and I don't get on. He believes I wasn't fit to shine Susan's shoes. He holds me responsible not only for her death but also for all of the other miseries in her life, including those she experienced before we met.'

Ray smiled. 'I had a girlfriend had a father like that.'

'So we don't speak. It's easier for both of us.'

'Let me ask you something else. You don't have to answer this question.'

'OK.'

'Why did Susan need Michael Conway?'

'Because Michael Conway is a good man – and Susan was always seduced by goodness because it was one of the few things she couldn't have. So I suppose she got the next best thing.'

'And this good man killed her?'

'So it would seem.'

'Why?' Ray said, leaning forwards again. 'Give me a motive.'

'Perhaps she asked him to. Perhaps she was playing with her gun and it went off. Perhaps he was playing with her gun and it went off. Don't you have a motive?'

Ray didn't answer that one, instead he said, 'We have enough to convict.'

'Good.'

'So where does that leave you?'

'I'm sorry?'

'She's looking for goodness in Michael Conway. She not get enough at home?'

'You can never get enough.'

He smiled. 'Tell me about Angela.'

'What do you want to know?'

'Did she have any reason to see your wife dead?'

'My wife, no. Me, yes.'

'Are you involved in a relationship with her?'

'Yes . . . mutual loathing.'

'Don't leave the city,' Ray said. He pulled on his jacket and walked out into the sun. I looked around the café: an uninspiring collection of caffeine addicts getting their morning fix. A sophisticate with his feet up on a cello case was drinking an iced latte. A woman with a poodle reading the *Village Voice* was eating ice cream from a sundae glass. I paid and walked out. A few doors down I found a grocery store where I bought two litre bottles of Coke and two 70cl bottles of Black Label. Then I walked back to the hotel to see Jordan.

18. Find the Olive

THREE DAYS AFTER the funeral I hadn't heard anything from Angela so after Michael's arrest I called round to see her. She was sharing an apartment with Carl off Lafayette Street. It was a messy, small place with a few art deco pieces of furniture, beaded curtains, ugly rugs, full ashtrays. It looked like a clairvoyant's parlour. Too dark for my tastes and cluttered with Carl's wooden boxes of records and belongings. Across the corridor somebody was playing a trad jazz record too loud. An argument was being shouted over it. Angela answered the door to me. Carl was out. She said I'd better come in and scratched her head as if she had lice. She looked like she'd just been asleep.

'What do you want?' She made no pretence at any kind of amicability.

'I thought we should talk.'

'I have nothing to say to you.' Angela slumped into a brown overstuffed chair and curled her legs beneath her.

'I thought you'd be curious about what the police had found out. But if you're not, then . . .' I shrugged and turned away. I was at the door before she called me back and asked me to sit down.

'I'm sorry, John Wayne, I'm trying not to feel angry at you but it's hard.'

'Then keep trying.'

She stared at me with the usual hate in her eyes.

I said, 'This is not about you, Angela. Don't you understand that?'

She laughed. 'Then I take it you imagine this is about you, do you?'

'Well, in the respect that Susan was my wife, then, yes, I have to say this is, to some degree, about me.'

'You're a pompous English asshole. You always were and you always will be. If you think you came anywhere close to the centre of Susan's life then you're a bigger fool than I thought you were. So, no, this is not to any degree about you. It never was.'

'Thanks.' I didn't go looking for sympathy from Angela, but I wasn't prepared for this.

'Don't take it personally.'

'I don't. I know how upset you are so I forgive you.'

'I don't need your forgiveness.'

'Nevertheless, I grant it to you.'

'You should have come to the wake. We stayed up all night and talked about our sister and when the sun rose we nearly came to find you.'

'To do what?'

'To do to you what you did to Susan.'

'And what do you imagine I did to Susan?'

'You imprisoned her and stole her spirit.'

'I did all that?'

'Yes.'

I said, 'And that's why you killed her is it?'

'Absolutely. I shot her through the heart to liberate her from you.'

'You know they arrested Michael Conway?'

'Yes.' Angela twisted round in her seat and took an apple from the glass bowl on the table behind her. She bit into it.

I said, 'Is that all you have to say?'

She didn't answer, just took another bite of the apple.

'Did they get the right man?'

'Any man will suffice.'

When we were in England, Susan and I escaped from Angela and the moron after I'd finally convinced him to take the train to Edinburgh. By this time Angela was, of course, denying that she'd agreed to this. She kept finding excuses to be alone with Susan; trying to make her see that we'd all have more fun if we stuck together. But Susan was becoming as tired of the moron as I was and she knew the only way to jettison him was also to jettison Angela. So she did and after we'd waved them off we booked into a country hotel.

It was our first night there. Susan was lying on the bed in a short white cotton night-dress. It wasn't that late but she was tired so we were eating a dinner of lemon chicken in the room and watching TV. The curtains were open. Huge arc lights lit up the velvet lawn. A softer yellow glow washed over the uneven terrace. The hotel was expensive and built in big blocks of Cotswold stone. It stood in a narrow valley which, according to the brochure, was within easy reach of Shakespeare Country and in the autumn and winter filled up with a river of mist twice a day (a nice Shakespearean touch by a copywriter who knew what he or she was doing – even though the way it was written made you feel that the hotel and not the valley got the mist).

For some reason we were talking about my mother. Susan said, 'I'd just like to understand why a woman called Wayne calls her son John.'

'It was a joke.'

'On you.'

'No. On everybody else.'

'How can the joke be on everybody else when people are laughing at you?' Susan laid her hands on her stomach, massaging Jordan whose progress from foetus to embryo we'd just toasted.

'They're not. They don't.' I sat beside her on the bed and put my hand on top of hers. 'When I tell people my name they wonder if I'm telling them the truth. That puts me at an immediate advantage.'

'I'm sorry?'

'Of course it does.'

'You meet somebody, tell them your name and immediately they question whether or not you're lying – and you think this puts you at an advantage?'

'Well . . . yes.'

'How twisted are you, John Wayne?' Susan lifted up my hand and ran her fingers over the palm, picking at the calluses with her fingernails. 'How twisted was she?'

'She wasn't twisted.'

'So defend her to me.'

'Defend her?'

'Yes.'

'I don't want to fight.'

Susan sat up and leaned back against the wall of lush pillows.

I said, 'I just don't want to spend all night arguing about my mother.'

'Now why do you assume I'm looking for an argument?'

'Because you are.' I stood up and went back to the window.

Susan waited for a moment, watching the silent TV, then she said, 'Then let's not argue. Let's talk.'

I said, 'It's interesting that immediately we start talking about my mother you ask me to defend her to you.'

'Is it?'

'I mean whose mother are we talking about here?'

'Fuck you, John Wayne.'

'You talk.'

She wouldn't. Instead, Susan found her glasses under the clutter on the bedside table and put them on. Depending on how vain she was feeling she sometimes used them for the TV. I picked up my book and sat in the loom chair in the wood-panelled window recess.

'I will, but not now,' she said after a while.

'OK.'

'I can't do it for other people. I have to do it for myself.'

'Yourself?'

'It's not a story yet.'

I put down my book and said, 'What?' But that seemed too harsh so I softened it, 'Do you want to explain that?'

'It hurts too much. When it stops hurting then I can tell it like a story. I'll know that when I can tell it as a story it won't hurt any more.'

'A story is something of yourself you give to somebody else?'

'Is that what I said?'

'I'm not sure.'

'When it stops hurting so much you try it out. Tell it in different ways. Each time you do it . . .'

'It gets easier.'

'It comes out a different way.'

'So stories are not for other people, they're for you?'

'They are also for other people. I have to stay selfish to protect myself.'

I went back to her, knelt on the floor by the high bed and peeled back the hem of her night-dress. Her stomach was only a little swollen. She looked at it like it belonged to somebody else, then she laid her hand on it again and repossessed herself.

I said, 'I was reading something.' I fetched the book and found the page. 'This is Philip Roth talking about writers . . .'

'Wait a minute.' Susan settled herself to listen and closed her eyes. 'OK. Ready.'

I read, 'I know writers. Beautiful feelings. They sweep you away with their beautiful feelings. But the feelings disappear quickly once you are no longer posing for them. Once they've got you figured out and written down, you go. All they give is their attention.'

'Go on.'

'That's all.'

'What is he saying? He's saying that people pose and writers write what they see. But that's not figuring people out, that's just observing the pose.'

I read it again. 'Depends on whether the feelings last beyond the pose. And it depends on the writer.' Susan took the book from me and flicked through it, twisting back the spine which I'd carefully preserved through 358 pages. I said, 'I marked it because it seemed to me to say something about my mother.'

Susan wasn't listening. Picking a speech, she read, 'I get angry when I want to get rid of somebody. They're in my way. Anger is a gun. I point it and I fire, and I keep firing till they disappear . . .'

'Are you angry?'

'At this moment?' She pulled off her glasses.

'Why are you always angry?'

'You don't know?'

'Do you want me to disappear?'

She pointed her finger and fired.

'Do you?'

'Not now . . .'

'When?'

'Is that how you feel?'

'Sometimes.'

Susan smiled. 'How did we get to this, John?'

'The wine. Being in England. Wondering why I was more surprised that you hadn't jumped into the river than I would have been if you had.'

'Would you have cared?'

'I'm not going to answer that.'

'Well think about why I posed the question, then consider if we're not asking the same of each other.'

I said, 'I do love you.'

'I know.' Then she softened. 'What does that passage say about your mother?'

'Reading it the first time seemed to mean something. It suddenly felt as though she'd lost interest.'

'And did she?'

'That's how it felt.'

'But she didn't lose interest in living.'

'No. Is that a criticism?'

'No.'

I said, 'Why did you marry me?'

'Because you asked.'

'Would you have married anybody who asked you?'

'How many more stupid questions are you going to ask me tonight?' She laid down the book and pulled off her night-dress. 'Find the olive,' she said.

That night in Susan's apartment, when she asked me to comment on her canvas and I returned the stolen photograph, you may recall the olives on the low table. Green olives. The next time I visited her apartment, she'd put out another bowl of them. I arrived bearing a bunch of roses. She took them, laid them on the counter, poured me a drink and led me to the centre of the room. She put down her glass, lifted her black dress to show she was entirely naked beneath, then let it drop. She opened her mouth to show that it was empty. She turned and lifted her dress again. Then she picked up an olive and told me to turn away. I duly did. She told me to turn back, then she said, 'Find the olive.'

It took three hours.

As I walked back to the hotel I wondered how long it took Michael Conway to find the olive. And where he found it.

19. George Gribbin's Rules
(The Agency – Afternoon)

AFTER SUSAN'S DEATH people said I should ease my way back to work. Angela said I should give it up altogether, live off the insurance and devote the rest of my life to bringing up Jordan. Possibly in a Kibbutz. She was walking round the apartment in a gypsy dress when she made this suggestion.

'Why?'

'Why not?'

'Did you come here solely to suggest that?' I said. This was our first conversation since I'd called in to see her. Jordan was at school and I was yet to tip fully over the rapids into alcohol dependency. I was, however, jittery and craving my first drink of the day.

'No, I came to see how you were.'

'Why?'

'Because I care about you.'

'No you don't.'

'Well I care about Jordan, therefore I have to care about you.'

She settled and rested against the wall. It must have been hard for her coming to the place where she'd spent so many evenings with Susan.

'Look, Angela. Let me get a drink. I'm trying to pretend to myself that I don't need one, but I do want one. So you can join me if you like, but if you don't then please don't give me a hard time about it or I'll have to ask you to leave.'

'Nice speech.'

I fetched a drink. When I came back into the room Angela was lifting a canvas off the wall. Two others were leaning against the couch. I said, 'Angela, what are you doing?'

'I'm taking the paintings back to the gallery.'

'What?'

'Susan didn't own them. She borrowed them.'

'All of them?'

'These. And that one there.'

She took down the fourth. The room looked bare, like a tree which had suddenly shed its leaves.

'This must be hard for you,' she said without sympathy.

'I think if you came here to help this is probably the worst thing you could have done.'

'Yes. I see that, and I'm sorry, John. Believe me, it hurts me as much as it hurts you.'

'You don't have to hate me now, Angela. Susan is dead. Somebody else is her best friend now.'

When she left with the paintings I moved the others around to try and cover the gaps but that just left more gaps so I took them all down and started again. Hanging pictures is hard but five hours later I decided I'd done the best I could. When Jordan came back from school and saw what I'd done he recoiled and insisted I let him re-do it. I watched him as he deftly moved the blocks of colour around until, quite quickly, he had the room balanced again and you would have been hard pushed to remember what it looked like before.

Susan, of course, took care of Jordan's art appreciation.

When he was old enough, the three of us would walk round Central Park on Sunday afternoons and she and Jordan would collect leaves and twigs and sometimes chocolate wrappers in a small bag. When we got home they'd tip their bounty onto the kitchen table and shuffle it around until they were both satisfied with the picture they had created. Sometimes it took hours, but they never kept the picture. An important part of the ritual was sweeping it away into a rubbish sack. Susan I think learned as much from Jordan as he did from her. I felt privileged watching them work and although there was no place for me in their game I wasn't resentful.

During the early post-funeral period, Susan's father, for once, offered the most useful advice. He told me that I would be of no use to Jordan, let alone myself, if I didn't have a job to go to. Coming from a man who put in fifteen hours a day when he was the sole custodian of his suicidal daughter, you had to wonder how valuable this advice was. Beneath it was his increasing concern over my drinking. He knew I couldn't drink at work, so being at work was probably a better thing than sitting in the apartment all day watching TV and getting fat.

Five weeks after the funeral, at around two-thirty one afternoon, I walked into the agency. The new girl at the desk didn't recognise me but before I had to explain who I was Chester saw me, terminated his phone call and came over to guide me into the room. He hugged me, steered me to my old chair, patted a cloud of dust from it and sat me down. He looked a little wired, moving and talking too fast. Angel was screaming at somebody in his office.

'Ottie,' Chester explained, diving back to his desk and sitting down.

I looked over at Michael's desk: no empty coffee cups, no photographs of Rosa and the girls, no newspaper cuttings spilling from his tray. Just a single carnation in a white vase, keyboard squared beneath the screen of the Power Mac 7500, witty screensaver, a box of white tissues with one, like a tiny frozen wave, spilling from the gash in the top, a stack of A4 manuals beneath a glass paperweight (an award of some description). Under the desk a wooden orthopaedic stool – more like a bird's perch than a chair.

'Where's Michael?' I said. I knew he'd been granted bail, which Ray told me was unusual but not so unusual when you employ the kind of legal representation that Michael had.

'He's at some hotel,' Chester said, then volunteered, 'Rosa came in and cleared his desk. Angel didn't ask her to but she said Michael wanted it that way . . . She said he'd be back after the trial.'

'Right. And in the meantime, he's brought in . . . what did you say her name was?'

'Ottie. German. Angel yells at her each day at around this time.' Chester smiled a tight smile. 'Ottie has yet to be reduced to tears by this. I recommended that she try it, then Angel might cut her some slack. Ottie says she has never resorted to tears and never will. If she doesn't I might.'

I pushed back in my chair, testing the backrest, then I reached underneath it for the lever which changed the height. The seat hissed and dropped an inch. The curled yellow post-it stickers round my screen meant nothing. I peeled them off and threw them away. In my desk drawer I found a cup of coffee scummed with green mould. I switched on my PC and the machine started its wake-up routine, the skin of the screen crackled and bristled with static electricity. The message light was flashing on my phone. I wiped the fourteen messages without listening to them. They belonged to another person who lived in another time.

'How's Jordan?' Chester called across.

'He's . . . he's confused,' I said.

Angel's door slammed open. 'John, you want to come in here, please?' And that was it. The end of the mourning. No fatherly hug. Not even a 'welcome back' or a 'good to see you'. Just Angel screaming at a young German girl who'd come, I soon learned, highly recommended from J. Walter Thompson by somebody whose judgement he had previously (but no longer) trusted. I knew it was serious because Angel had resorted to 'Mr George Gribbin's five rules' which meant we were going 'back to fucking basics'. Angel, who happened to have studied under the great man himself, could still repeat verbatim the great man's history as well as his finest copy.

George Homer Gribbin was born in Michigan in 1907, went to journalism school at the University of Wisconsin but transferred to study English at Stanford. He failed to get into his preferred career – journalism – but found his way into the fledgling advertising industry. He worked for a few department stores before he was hired by Macy in New York. From there, in 1935, he moved to Young and Rubicam as a copywriter. Sometime during this period Angel came under his wing. According to the legend as Angel tells it, Gribbin took to the younger man and shared his enthusiasm for luminaries such as Sid Ward and Ted Patrick with him. Angel, like many successive copywriters, ate it up. Gribbin was a great teacher as well as being a great writer. Within twenty-five years he was president and the agency was the third largest in the USA.

'Five rules,' Angel announced and began to deliver them, pacing three steps, turning, pacing three steps back. 'One.' He hooked the little finger of his right hand onto the little finger of his left. 'Find the picture that draws the eye to the headline. Two.' First finger of right hand pulling down third finger of left. 'Write a headline that makes the prospect want to read the first line of the copy. Three.' Ditto with fourth finger of left. 'Write a first line that makes you want to read the second. Four. Continue this process until the end. Five. Make the words and picture add up to something that makes the prospective customer want to reach their hands into their pockets and buy.' He looked at me, then Ottie, then back at me. Ottie was looking out of the window. 'You listening to me, young lady?'

'I'm listening.'

Ottie's copy for 'Kool Kat' – a dumpy refrigerator in a range of primary colours, with 50s retro styling – was folded on Angel's desk. He handed it to me. Now she had a chance to see whether I mattered, Ottie's attention was back in the room. She'd used Quark to mock-up a full-page advert with a few lines of copy at the bottom. The whole thing had a period feel, right down to the Doris Day/Rock Hudson figures and dialogue at the bottom. I could see what she was doing and I knew why Angel didn't like it. People who've lived through difficult times don't appreciate those periods being lampooned, however fondly.

I said, 'What are you asking?'

Angel took back the sheet and tore it in half. 'I'm asking whether you would be kind enough to speak to this young lady and explain to her the way I like things done.'

'Fine,' Ottie said, and walked out.

I waited, but Angel was back at his desk, head down, muttering to himself and poking through some letters. I closed the door on him.

People like Ottie with their *screw-you* sneers make me feel old. Nothing fazes them. They wait to be impressed by you rather than the other way round, watching you like TV, the remote in their hands, waiting to switch you off. Angel sees it as the young exhibiting a lack of respect for their elders (young being anybody under twenty-five). I argued that this was only partially true. They have respect, but they don't award it wantonly like we did. Getting old does not in itself any longer warrant applause. In fact, unless you're unlucky, it is easier to get old than it used to be and the young know it. After all, the elderly are more prone to stupidity than the young and have less of an excuse. Angel is at his worst when he lapses into solipsism. As are we all, I expect.

I took Ottie to a bar and offered her a drink. She didn't, as I'd expected, coyly ask for a bottle of fizzy water or a Diet Coke, she joined me with a Scotch but accepted the water jug I'd declined. We sat in a booth. Ottie fetched out a pack of Winston cigarettes. Two vices, even better. She offered one to me. I took it. On our way there we'd been through the recent history: how long she'd been there, what she thought of Chester ('OK' – high praise indeed), what she'd heard about Angel and the agency before she accepted the job (small but significant, plenty of responsibility but limited financial rewards, forward thinking but conservative, worthy of a year or so there before stepping back on a higher rung of the ladder at a larger agency). The earlier history was for another time or never.

Ottie said, 'I studied Gribbin.' German Ottie with her soft accent, black wood-framed glasses, eager blue eyes, olive unblemished skin. Petite; stylish; now. A girl James Stewart would have taken the glasses from and said, 'But you're beautiful.'

I said, 'So did we all.'

'So what is the big deal?'

'Angel likes rules. They make him feel safe.'

'He resorts to rules when he feels threatened?'

'Something like that.'

Ottie took a sip of the Scotch. She drank it down in a way

that I knew she was doing it to keep me company. There was nothing habitual about it.

'Your wife was murdered?' she said in the same tone she used when she asked how long I'd been in New York.

'Yes.'

'By Michael Conway?'

'So it would seem.'

'. . . Forgive me for saying this, but you sound unconvinced.'

'No. I'm convinced.'

Ottie took another tentative sip. She said, 'I believe I know Michael Conway quite well.'

'How?'

'He was good. I looked through his work.'

'Michael was good.'

'You can learn about people through their work.'

'So you never met him?'

'Yes. He called me and asked if we could meet.'

'And?'

'We met.' A pause. 'What are we doing here, John?'

'You're today's winner in my drinking companion competition.'

'OK.' Ottie didn't load any judgement onto this. 'I expect I should ask you what you thought about my Kool Kat idea.'

'Do you really want to know?'

'Honestly? No.'

'OK. I'll tell you. And I'll give you my opinion – not Angel's. They differ but if you go with mine you'll be OK with Angel. If you go with Angel you won't necessarily be OK with me. You'll have to decide for yourself which you consider the most useful.'

Ottie was watching me but she'd stopped listening. 'You should not be back at work,' she said. 'It is too soon.'

'You don't know me.'

'I can see you.'

'Tell me what Michael said when you met him. When did you meet him?'

'Two days ago.'

'And why did he want to meet?'

'Because he wanted somebody to convince of his innocence. Somebody he did not know but had a valid reason for meeting.'

'And were you convinced?'

'I think this is a conversation you should be having with him, don't you?'

'Probably not.' I took her hand and she didn't flinch. 'Do you know what I'd really like?'

'Tell me.'

'To sleep.'

Ottie took my fingers in her mouth and sucked them: slowly: slowly: in. Out. In. Deep into her hot warm mouth. Too much sensation throughout my whole body to be able to talk. I tried until Ottie shushed me, telling me that this is what her mother did when she was a child to help her sleep. I closed my eyes. In. Out. In. Slow, slow; rhythm like waves, like wind blowing over a field of corn, like . . . like . . .

'Wake up.' A gentle voice I didn't know calling me back to the shore. I opened my eyes and looked around the bar. On the circular table before me the detritus of a snack meal. Three empty glasses, another holding a measure of Scotch. A full ashtray. The dandruff of ash all over the table. Other senses. The smell of a perfume I didn't know. The sound of a TV far, far away in the corner of a room and a slow conversation between the barman and a man who'd come to fill the cigarette machine. I felt the warmth of a woman I now knew I was leaning against.

'I'm sorry,' I said.

'We should go back,' Ottie said.

I looked at my watch. 5.18.

'And please don't tell Angel that we slept together.'

'I won't. Thank you, Ottie.'

The next evening I met Michael Conway in the Oyster Bar at Grand Central Station. His idea. Ottie had a telephone number for the Chelsea hotel he was staying in. The first thing he said when he answered was that Rosa had asked him to move out until the trial was over. When he started puzzling it through: telling me that he didn't kill Susan, couldn't understand why I thought he did, stumbling through his words like a drunk, I stopped him and said we should meet. He said his lawyer had told him on no account should he see me but I was the only person he felt he could trust. I think that was the first time it all came home to me. Of all the people involved in this story only two people really mattered: me and Michael Conway and it was Michael Conway who mattered the most. The court case could proceed without me.

I beat Michael there by five minutes. When I saw him being led between the tables towards me I didn't recognise him. It could have been an old, down-on-his-luck writer meeting his agent. The man's mac was filthy, he needed a shave, there was a rash on his face. Closer to, when I saw it was Michael, I saw the focused, mad Michael you sometimes got when he was in the white-heat of creativity.

'How did we get here, John? How did we get to be here?' Michael leaned down and embraced me. His coat was damp. His breath smelt like death. He was carrying a newspaper and a bundle of handwritten notes rolled together like filthy dollars. He hung on until I managed to pull my arm from out of his bear hug, and reached up to pat him twice on the shoulder. He released the clench. The waiter waited for his coat.

'Oh, yes. Yes. Yes.' Michael pulled off his mac and the man took it and left the lunatics in peace. Michael sat down, looked around him and leaned in. 'Thank you for calling. I was waiting. I knew you would. I couldn't call you. You understand? I couldn't call you.' He poured himself a glass of water from the iced jug on the table. His hands shook. All of the ice cubes fell into his glass. 'Dry mouth.' He touched his lips feverishly. 'The drugs my doctor gave me. Be aware they may make your mouth dry, he said. They did.' A weak self-pitying smile, eyes full of tears. 'Consciousness is a highly overrated condition. How did we get here, John? How in God's name did we get to be here?'

I said, 'Susan was shot dead. That's how we got here.'

His mouth opened, trying to form the words. It suddenly struck me we should have met at Mort's. Michael managed, 'I did not kill Susan. You know that, John.' He pressed his case with the force and control of his voice. The waiter arrived at the moment he raised his voice to repeat the sentiment. 'I did not kill your wife.'

The waiter cleared his throat. 'Would you gentlemen like to order a drink?'

'I'll have another Scotch. Make that two,' I said, and the waiter went.

'It's very important to me that you believe this. I can't tell you how important this is.'

'Why should I believe you?'

'Because it's true. And you know that it is. I can see that you know it is.'

'You were in the apartment.'

'Yes. But when I left she was alive.'

'You were having an affair with Susan.'

'I loved her. Why should I murder . . . ?'

I reached over the table and slapped him hard on the side of the face. It sobered some of the madness out of him. I thought he was going to cry with the shock. I thought I was going to puke with the mean little image I saw of it in my mind. A slap around the face for a man who'd been sleeping with my wife: what kind of gesture was that?

'Look at this . . .' Michael was holding up his hands, pulling his fingers apart. There were cracks between each one. 'I have a rash all over my body. My skin falls off me when I take a shower.' And then, as if his reactions lagged, 'I can understand why you hit me. I don't blame you for hitting me.'

'Thanks.'

'Hit me again if it'll make you feel any better.'

'I might do that.'

'Fine. Fine . . . there's not much time for me now, John.'

'Order some food.'

'I can't eat.'

'Order something or we'll have to leave and I don't want to leave just yet.'

When the drinks came we managed to order a couple of dozen Cape Cod oysters and a bottle of house wine. Michael pulled out a pen from his trouser pocket and jotted something down on one of his scraps of paper.

'Are you taking notes?'

'I'm just trying to remember everything about that night. My lawyer recommended I write each thing down as I remember it. I wake in the night and I remember something else. I write it down. That's when I can sleep. The hotel is noisy. People coming in and out all night. Sometimes I phone Rosa and the girls. She leaves the machine on but I call her just so I can hear her voice. She won't talk to me. I can't blame her but it's very hard not seeing my babies.' More tears spilled out of him.

'So what did you just remember?'

Michael wiped his eyes and consulted his sheet. 'I wrote down that I remembered feeling guilty about you when I went up to the apartment.'

I snatched the paper away from him. Michael tried to pull it back and tore the corner. I turned away from him so I could read it. Ink blots, a few words and phrases unconfined by the faint blue lines on the spiral pad paper. 'Cab fare. Something, something, Rosa's birthday. Receipt. Leave John. Promise.'

'Give it back to me please.'

'What is this?'

'Please. Give it back to me.'

'Leave John. Promise.'

'John. Listen to me.'

'Explain to me what this means: Leave John. Promise.'

'Just listen. Listen and I'll explain.'

'Explain.'

Michael held out his hand. I gave him back his piece of paper. He rolled it round the others and put it in his trouser pocket.

'Can I please have some more water?'

I poured him another glass. He lifted it two-handed to his mouth then set it carefully back on the cloth.

'This is how I saw it. I figured it like this. If you rang I knew you believed I didn't kill Susan.'

'Leave John. Promise. Explain that to me.'

'Wait. Just listen to me. Please. John. I know that you're hurt. OK. I can't know just how hurt you are because I cannot imagine how I'd feel if something like this happened to . . .'

'Rosa? Try and imagine something else. Insert another name into your imagining.'

'Please . . . I'm trying to help both of us here.'

The waiter sailed up, holding a bottle of wine, label to the front, bottom angled forwards. 'Would you like to try the wine, sir?'

'Just pour it.'

'Very good, sir.'

He pulled the cork and filled the glasses, twisting the bottle each time to cut off the flow. Then he bedded it deep into the ice lining the silver bucket and dropped a starched white cloth over the neck. He bowed away.

'I know you know I didn't kill Susan.'

'What is this leading to?'

Michael tried to compose himself. He'd been working up to this and he didn't want to get it wrong. 'We need to find out who did.'

'Leave John. Promise.'

'No. Listen. Listen to me. I know you hate me, John. And I can't blame you for that. But I know that you're a good man.' I laughed. 'No. I know that you are and I can't believe, deep in my heart, that you'd want the wrong person to go to jail for the murder.'

'It's out of my hands, Michael.'

'Don't tell me you have no influence over this because I don't believe it.'

'I have no influence over this.'

'Please. If only for Susan . . .'

'Susan's dead. What does she care?'

'Who killed Susan, John?'

'You did.'

'No.'

'Leave John. Promise.'

'OK.' Michael pulled out his scraps. 'If this is what you want. Is this what you want?'

I sat back and thought. No. I didn't think this was what I wanted, but it was too late. Michael was reading out from his scraps. 'Called her from the agency. 5 p.m. John working late. Agree to meet. Jordan answers door. He goes out. Susan undoes my trousers. She isn't wearing underwear. We didn't talk, we went straight through to the . . . Is this what you want?'

'Fuck you.'

'I'm sorry.' Bunching the scraps together again. 'You agreed to meet me. That's what gave me hope, John. I know you know I didn't kill her. If you thought I did you wouldn't have agreed.'

'So who did?'

'I have some ideas.'

'Some?'

He searched the room again then pulled his chair closer to the table. 'I told the detective this but he didn't want to know. Like he'd already made his mind up.' He waited, wanting to see how I felt about this. All I could see was Ray leaning towards me across another table and asking me to give him a motive.

'Go on.'

'Angel.'

'Yes, sure. Try again.'

'Chester.'

'What about Rosa? You haven't mentioned Rosa yet.'

'Rosa wasn't asked to visit Angel's parties and I wouldn't have wanted her there. Believe me. She would not have understood.'

'You're telling me Chester went to Angel's parties?'

'Yes.'

'OK. And so did you?'

'You had to be a part of it, John. We had no choice.'

'He never asked me.'

'This was before you joined the agency. Then Angel

162

started to worry. He couldn't control it. Too many people. Unsafe. A couple of girls got hurt. But everybody was there.'

'Susan?'

'. . . Yes. Of course, Susan. She was part of the scene. You had to be.'

'Give me a motive.'

'I can't.' He slumped back, spent. 'I thought you'd . . . I mean, I thought together we could . . .'

'Listen,' I said. Michael lit up, sensing some hope. 'When they put you in jail for killing Susan do you know what I'm going to do?'

'What?'

'I'm going to take the train from Grand Central Station and I'm going to get off at your stop. Then I'm going to get a cab and ask him to drive me slowly through your suburb. Round and round so I can get to know the streets. Taste them. Taste how they feel. And when I know them I'm going to call on Rosa and offer my sympathy. Take her some flowers, a bottle of wine, and then we're going to drink it. Maybe another. Do you have wine in your cellar? And then . . .'

'No.'

'No. Listen. And then, by now I don't know, it may be midnight. I'll make sure it is. And I'll say – Oh my God, I've missed the last train home, looking at my watch to make it more authentic – and she'll say that's OK John, you can stay the night. Yes Michael?'

He was twisting the silver wedding ring on his finger now, eyes vacant: there; imagining.

'How does she like it, Michael? Do you want to give me some tips?'

Michael was rocking like a lunatic, twisting, twisting his ring on his cracked fingers.

'Do you like to turn her over?'

'Please.'

'Yes? Turn her over and give it to her up the ass?'

Michael stood up, pushing his chair away. A couple of waiters stopped what they were doing. The chair dropped onto its back. Three, four, five faces turned our way. More. Then everybody when the glass fell off the table and shattered. It really should have been Mort's. How to describe Michael's face. Hate? No. Horror? A moment before, but not now. Defeat? Yes. Defeat.

'I never believed it,' he said. 'I never believed you did it.'

He walked out through the vaults, leaving his coat behind him again. Ottie was right. It was too soon to go back to work.

20. Goodbye Carol

WHEN WE GOT back from Yellowstone Park we unloaded the VW at the apartment. It was a silent and sad task. Folded in the canvas were the memories of our race to get the tent up, the meals we'd eaten from our knees and the daily tussle to get out of washing up, the nights we'd slept a few feet apart, waking when the rain started beating on the fabric, unzipping and looking out as the earth turned to mud and not caring. Being glad, even, because we were warm and dry and the elements couldn't touch us. But, more than anything, the miracle I'd experienced: 'Dear Cynthia,' I wrote in my head, 'I learned to live for the day again and my son taught me how to do it.'

Jordan and I had found a way to talk, but after the episode with Mary the peg lady and her girls the trip had gone sour. Jordan blamed me for it and I blamed myself. We'd arrived back in the city trailing the cloud of Susan's death over the van like a kite. When we got back to the apartment after dropping off the van, Jordan went straight to his room and closed the door. I looked through the stack of mail: a letter from the insurance company and one from Angela addressed in red ink to 'my godson, Jordan Wayne' – she no longer communicated with me directly. She'd drawn butterflies on the back of the envelope around the returning address. There were also three bills and a postcard from a friend of Jordan's. I decided to call Carol.

I'd intended to do this while we were away but after the call from Cody there was nothing I wanted to say to her and I didn't want to make things worse between us. I needed her in the city. I did not need her anywhere else. I tried her mobile, but it was dead so I tried her at home. If Steve picked up the phone I'd pretend I'd got a wrong number. A woman answered. I took a chance and said, 'Is Carol there?'

She said, 'Who is this, please?'

'I'm a friend of Carol.'

'It's you, isn't it?'

'Is Carol there?'

'No. Carol is not here.' The woman was angry.

'OK. I'll try her later.'

'Do you know how much damage you've caused?'

'Is this about the shelves I built for Steve?'

Only a moment's pause as she processed the possibility, then, 'I'm Steve's sister and I'm sitting the apartment for them.'

'I'll call some other time.'

'Are you not concerned about them?'

'Look. I don't want to be rude, Ms . . .'

'Gil.'

'Gil, but I called to speak to Carol so you'll have to excuse me, I have other things to do.' But of course I was intrigued. Ms Gil talked with the same prosaic pedantry as her brother. Wounded and outraged: another city victim like me.

'My brother and Carol are travelling round Europe in a bid to salvage their marriage.'

'OK, I'll call when they get back.'

'Twenty-two years of happy marriage and then you came along and spoiled everything for them.'

166

'Yes, happy, right.'

'I'd like to slap your face, Mr Wayne.'

'Carol used to do that. She'd slap me, then hug me, slap me, then hug me. I love you, I hate you, I love you, I hate you. Like that. It was a game we had. Perhaps she was pretending to be you, Ms Gil.'

'If I didn't know something of your history I'd find you offensive. Because I do, you'll have to forgive me for not taking the bait.' There was nothing to say to that so she asked, 'Are you drunk?'

'No more than usual.'

'Leave her alone. Leave them both alone, or you'll have me to answer to.'

'And what line of work are you in Ms Gil?'

'Thank you for calling and goodbye.' With that she put the phone down.

Jordan wandered through the room and into the kitchen. He pulled open the fridge looking for snacks. Seeing nothing there he slammed it again.

'We need to shop,' I said.

'Great.' Jordan vaulted onto the counter and sat there, dangling his legs and looking through the wad of mail, his hair flopping down over his face. The trip had given him some colour in his cheeks. Before the setback with Mary he was even occasionally managing eye-contact as we talked. He read the card that was addressed to him, then dropped it onto the floor. He opened the insurance letter that was addressed to me, scanned it, and lost interest. The letter from Angela he slipped into his back pocket then he slapped the remaining pile down beside him.

I said, 'Are you going to open that?'

'No. Who were you talking to?'

'Some woman.'

'Carol?'

'What?'

'Were you talking to Carol?'

'No. Carol who?'

'Dad. Pleeease.'

Jordan jumped down and pulled open a wall cupboard. He reached up and slipped a box of cereals out of the tight clutch of the others next to it. Looking in the fridge and seeing there was no milk, he delved his hand inside the packet and fisted a dry mouthful of wheatflakes into his mouth. All of this while I was trying to take in the fact that he knew about Carol.

'What do you know about Carol?' I said.

'Not much.'

'So . . . ?'

'It's no big deal. I don't expect you to live like a . . . like a man who lives on his own all the time.'

'A hermit?'

'No. A religious monk.'

'Well . . . well, fine. Thanks.'

'No problemo.'

'. . . Did Angela tell you?'

'No.'

'. . . Did you tell Angela?'

'Maybe.'

Jordan sauntered out clutching the packet of Weetos. The cold war seemed to be over for a while. I called Carol's number again. Ms Gil answered.

'Ms Gil,' I said.

'Yes.'

'It's me again. Him.'

'Listen to me. I'd really much prefer if we had no further communication. It can serve no purpose. Thank you for calling.'

Not as tight-assed as I'd first thought. Some amusement

now in her voice. I thought she was probably bored and, like me, looking for some diversion.

I said, 'Perhaps we should meet.'

'Mr Wayne. I can assure you I have no intention of ever setting eyes on you. It would serve no purpose whatsoever. More than that, it would undoubtedly compromise my relationship with both my brother and his wife. I do not wish to get involved. Now please stop calling me.'

'They don't need to know. Do you think I want to make Carol's life any harder for her?'

'Well . . .'

'Whatever you may have been told, Ms Gil, I was extremely fond of Carol. I won't say that I loved her because I'm sure if I did, you'd say I was lying. However, she is, or at least was, very important to me. So her welfare remains one of my highest priorities.' Jordan came in to say something. I turned my back on him on the pretext of jotting something down on a sheet of paper. He walked up to the paper, looked pointedly at the scribble, raised his eyebrows and went back to his room.

'I'm glad to hear that,' Ms Gil was saying.

'Do you like Carol?'

'What . . . ?'

'Just answer, do you like Carol?'

'Yes. I have a great deal of time for Carol.'

'And do you occasionally seek her opinion? Say, if you're buying a new dress or something, and you don't want your husband to be involved, in fact you want to surprise him with . . .'

'I'm not married, Mr Wayne.'

Of course you're not. 'All right, you're out on a date and . . .'

'I really don't see where this is leading.'

'It's leading to me asking you whether you value Carol's opinion.'

'Yes. Of course I value her opinion.'

'OK. So let's put this another way.' Ms Gil sighed, but she knew I was expecting a token demurral at this point. 'Please hear me out.'

'Do hurry up.'

'OK. So, if you value Carol's opinion you must ipso facto trust her judgement.'

'I'll concede that to you.'

'And she chose me so the chances are you'd like me too.'

'Mr Wayne. In life there are, I'm sure, a million people we'd all like if we had the good fortune to meet them. There are also a great number that, for reasons which are out of our hands, we can never meet. Now, whether you fall into the former category is academic because there is no question that you fall into the latter.'

I said, 'Are you aware of Project Read?'

'Project Read?'

'Yes. In a city of something like two hundred languages or dialects . . .'

She cut in. 'Listen to me.'

'OK. I'm listening.'

'Mr Wayne, I hope you won't take this wrongly, but I have had some experience with the recently bereaved.'

'That doesn't surprise me.'

'Anger is a common . . .'

'Ms Gil, I hope *you* won't take this wrongly, but the world is full of people like you – and they have always had experience with the recently bereaved, or the suicidal, or the plain no-nonsense fucked up.'

'Mr Wayne . . .'

'And when these people listen to the voice of reason, because you are that plaintive voice, they say to themselves:

Heavens Above – I'm listening to the voice of reason, perhaps the world is not so bad after all . . .'

'I should . . .'

'. . . Because people like you are just so reasonable you force people to pretend they have been cured just so they don't offend you – OK? They do not want to offend the voice of reason. And what this makes them do is to go home and drink the pain away, or bury it, or abuse their neighbours, or their children or beat their wife, or . . . I don't know, do something so grotesquely unreasonable . . .'

'Anger, Mr Wayne . . .'

'Say?'

'What you are feeling now is . . .'

'Do not presume to tell me what I am feeling. Never presume to tell me what I am feeling. You. You and the other voices of reason are more dangerous than the most brutal murderer because you live vicariously, OK? All of your experience is vicarious. Who do you visualise when you masturbate, Ms Gil?'

'In with the good – out with the bad.'

'Because Carol masturbated all the time. But she pretended not to with Steve because she thought it would offend him. She didn't want to offend your brother – another voice of reason. He has a very small penis, apparently. Do you still value Carol's opinion? I wonder if you should when she's told me – a practical stranger – that.'

'You really are a very disturbed individual.'

'Hey – listen Ms Gil. I have your address. I have it, all right? Are you alone right now because if you are I'd recommend that you rectify that situation immediately.'

'Did you get your son back?'

'What?'

'Carol mentioned that your son was removed by the ACS.'

'Yes, I got my son back.'

'I'm so glad to hear that.'

She put the phone down on me again. When I tried the number I got the engaged tone. What I did with the energy was to kick out two of the doors in the kitchen. They splintered. One of them had a rack of preserves screwed to the back of it. The sticky red mess sludged out onto the floor. Shards of glass ledged in it like a miniature tableau of a shark attack.

One more call. I promised I'd get in touch with Ray when I got back from the trip. I'd also been putting off this conversation but with Carol gone, it seemed fitting somehow to lay Susan's ghost finally to rest. I felt as though I was coming out of the darkness. This wasn't a smooth ride, some days I lurched back in again, but I was getting glimpses of another life: a lighter world that predated Susan's death, perhaps even predated Susan. Here was a less complex life where I could be who I was without reference to her. I called the First Precinct and asked to be put through, but the nasal woman on the switchboard said Ray was no longer working there. I asked where I could reach him and she said he'd just been transferred to the South Brooklyn Homicide Squad. Good for Ray, I said, he got what he wanted. She asked how I knew Ray and we had a short conversation about him. In the course of it I learned that he was married and that he was highly regarded by everybody who came into contact with him. He was also the union delegate for the precinct, so they were looking to replace him and it was going to be a difficult job. The woman said it was good to talk to me, she rarely got the opportunity to talk to people nowadays. People were always in such a hurry and since she and her husband split she could go all day without talking to anyone for more than thirty seconds. (Fifteen years of marriage, she said, but they just seemed to lose interest in each other. He was a heavy smoker – sometimes three packs a day – and since she herself gave up under hypnosis she couldn't stand the smell on his clothes.) I said I supposed her job was difficult in that respect. People who call the police department usually do so for a reason, not like, say, calling a company to come and quote them for a new kitchen. You'd be surprised, she said, at some of the things people call for. She'd just put the phone down on a woman who wanted to know what time it was in Kuala Lumpur. If people called with an enquiry, by now she had so many numbers in her head she'd decided it made her job more interesting to give them out and listen for people's reactions rather than just saying she didn't know. In fact she had something of a photographic memory for numbers.

Finally she gave me Ray's number but when I called it they said he wasn't in and promised to give him a message. The man on the phone was hard to read. He gave nothing away and I knew Ray was moving in a tougher world now.

The court case against Michael Conway was 'posited on a number of rotten planks of evidence'. (His eager young lawyer said this early on – it didn't help. The ancient, dyspeptic judge looked at him like a new fashion he didn't approve of.) Ray went to Michael's arraignment, just to see it safely through, he said. When it came to court, Michael's lawyer decided on a jury trial which at least gave him control of who was going to sit in judgement. They had the evidence of the superintendent which put him inside the building. They had the condom, which put him, however briefly, inside Susan. And they had the fingerprints on Susan's gun. This was the biggest point of contention. Michael's lawyer argued that on the SAFIS analysis alone there were any number of other people who could have pulled that trigger: Jordan's pawmarks were on there, mine were, as were Angela's and Susan's. But the man under scrutiny was Michael. Unfortunately for him, the prosecutor swatted Michael's lawyer's summation away with some nicely timed put-downs – 'Was he suggesting, perhaps, that Jordan shot his mother in cold blood?' This raised the only laugh of the five-day trial, quickly stifled. The question, of course, was rhetorical and Michael's lawyer had the good sense to keep his prematurely balding head down so the jury couldn't see the answer on his tired face. A couple of days before he'd also dispensed with the rest of us: alibis for me and Angela (working late – mine, and Lilith Fair – Angela). Several thousand women could be called to support Angela's alibi, I just had Angel. But it wasn't necessary to get him involved on this point. He had, however, been called by the defence as a character witness. Angel relished the spotlight. He'd decided to play the wise elder spokesman. He took his time getting to the witness box, pausing as he reached it to get his breath back. He declaimed his name so loudly into the microphone that the public address system started whistling and continued to do so until a court official managed to find the amplifier and turn it down. Then, when he spoke, he spoke slowly, as if Michael was his only son: a boy he'd nurtured, given the best years of his life to, but who had, unfortunately, taken a wrong turn. He made it clear that Michael was not a bad man. Under cross-examination from the prosecutor he was forced to concede that Michael was occasionally hot-headed and passionate. At the agency he'd seen him on his wilder days when words spilled out of him and he couldn't seem to control himself. We were left to feel, as Angel stepped down, that Michael had just – possibly at the height of passion – gone a little too far and pulled the trigger on a gun. All supposition, of course, but when he was called, what could Chester do but agree?

What I was waiting for was Michael's one big chance –

Angel's parties. If his defence team brought up the whole murky Sodom of wild nights in Gramercy Park, then I knew Michael must surely have a chance. Except it was never mentioned. I could not believe it. Until I thought it through and the only logical reason seemed to be that Rosa never knew about Angel's parties and, ultimately, Michael believed he was going to be convicted of Susan's murder and he wanted at least to preserve something of his reputation – if only for the family. So he kept it back and, in so doing, he wasn't also flayed for taking part in masked orgies at which a number of women were hurt, drugs were consumed, and bodies of all colours and several sexes intertwined for forty-eight-hour periods. An adulterous Manhattan manslaughter would warrant a few brief prurient paragraphs in the newspapers: maybe an op/ed piece motivated by *schaden-freude*. Add in a Rabelaisian romp and the feature coverage would run for weeks.

In many ways, Michael's lawyer had an easier job than the prosecutor. He had to raise sufficient doubts in the minds of the jury that Michael had pulled the trigger. He'd done this by focusing on Michael's character: his exemplary record, his career, his more memorable campaigns. Then he swung round to look at the jury and asked which one among them was free from sin? A man blushed. A woman nodded.

The judge then read the jury charge and laid out the salient parts of the criminal code for the benefit of the jurors. He shook his arms free from his black loose-sleeved cape, looked over his half-moon glasses, and gravely read out the options: murder of the first degree, second degree, voluntary manslaughter, involuntary manslaughter. I looked round at Rosa as the judge was saying: 'Criminal homicide constitutes voluntary manslaughter when a person voluntarily, upon a sudden heat of passion, fights with and kills another person.' Rosa was clenching and unclenching her hands as if she was wringing out a sheet, sitting slightly forwards in her seat. '. . . Involuntary manslaughter when a person unguardedly or undesignedly kills another human being . . .'

The jury was out for two hours and when they filed back, a verdict of voluntary manslaughter was returned. Michael held his head in his hands and cried like a baby. Rosa stood up and reached out as if somehow she could hold him. He looked at her through the tears, and the courtroom was silent. He was taken down, looking back just once at her. I moved towards Rosa. I think he saw me, because he flinched and at that moment I remembered how we'd parted and what I had said to him under the vaults of the Oyster Bar. I didn't mean to add to his misery.

Outside, after the reporters, I found myself walking down the street with Rosa. Both victims now, it seemed only fitting that we should share our sorrows. I tried to talk to her but she didn't seem to want to. She didn't resist when I took her arm and steered her into a bar. We sat on tall stools and I asked her what she wanted to drink, then she came to life, insisting on getting them and fumbling in her purse for her money.

'It's all right,' I said, putting my hand on hers. 'I'll get them.' Let me do this for you, I wanted to say. You don't have to take charge of your life yet. Leave it a few more hours.

'No. I have some money in here.' She upended her purse on the bar. A bunch of keys jangled out, a rape alarm, a small box of tampons, two virgin tissues, lipstick, a car park receipt. A man's wallet. She picked the wallet out of the pile and pulled out a ten-dollar bill, handing it over to the barman after he put the drinks in front of us on two paper coasters. It was Michael's wallet, I recognised it, the tan worn smooth by countless back pockets. It was curved slightly from living so close to him.

'Thanks,' I said. Rosa picked up her glass and drank down her vodka. She gasped, opened her eyes wide, put the glass on the bar and called for another. The barman looked at me, which Rosa didn't appreciate. He was a squat, blue-collar pugilist from the Ed Asner school of world-weariness. Not just a barman, he had the presence of somebody who owned the place and his attitude was bereft of subservience.

Rosa said, 'I'm over here.'

The man conceded with a curt nod and a quick reappraisal of the lady in the knee-length black skirt, black jacket and white blouse.

'You fuck,' Rosa said under her breath. The man heard, debated whether to take her on, and decided it wasn't worth it. He put the second vodka in front of her and took his frustration out on the old-fashioned till which he elbowed hard to open. In other circumstances I expect this was one of his party tricks: a smile, a quick elbow on the button, the tray shoots out, he gets the change and bellies the tray closed, all in the blink of an eye. The barman handed Rosa her change with no smile and went back to his newspaper which was spread out on the side bar.

'To Michael Conway,' Rosa said, looked at the drink, high in her hand, and drank it down as if it was Michael she was drinking.

'Michael,' I said, and took a sip. I saw him stumbling out of the Oyster Bar without his coat.

Rosa was looking hard at me. 'What's the matter with you? You got what you wanted, didn't you?'

'Did I?'

'I told Michael the lawyer was wrong. The judge thought he was a fool. He was a fool.'

I knew anything I could say would only make things worse so I said nothing. Rosa leaned her elbows on the bar and dry-washed her face with her palms. She muttered something, but it was inaudible.

'Who did it, John?'

'I don't know.'

'But not Michael. Michael didn't do it. Was it you?'

'I thought you knew me, Rosa.' I waved my glass at the barman. Irritated, he sauntered over, took my glass and poured another measure into it, then put it down in front of me. I went for my money. He waved it away and said, 'Put it on a tab.' Then back to his newspaper.

'I never loved Michael,' Rosa said. 'But I wouldn't have wished this on him.'

'Nobody would.'

'So what do I do now?'

'I . . .'

'I don't want to know.'

'OK.'

'That weekend, when Michael and I stayed in your apartment . . .'

'Yes?'

'It started then, right?'

'I don't know.'

'I spent a hundred and seventy-five dollars on a dress yesterday.'

'Right.'

'I should take it back.'

'. . .'

'I went to my hairdresser this morning and she asked me what I wanted and I said, "Cut my hair short, short like Hillary Clinton." She said, "Are you sure?" Because this woman has been cutting my hair for seven years and she knows I am prone to changing my mind. And I said, "No I'm not sure." And she said, "OK, so what would you like me to do with it?" So I said, "Just do the usual."'

She ran her hands through her stiff hair.

'And she said, "Mrs Conway, would you come this way please?" And she took me over to the sink and I leaned back against the . . . the porcelain and felt the warm water on my hair, saturating it, the woman just, she said, "How is the temperature for you?" "Fine." . . . So she massaged my scalp and it was so soothing I slept for a minute or so. And when I woke up I'd forgotten everything. No court case. No Michael falling apart in a hotel room. Just Rosa Conway getting her hair washed ready for the weekend, kids safe at school . . . everything . . . safe. A list of things to fetch from the stores. Those decisions you take for . . . my mother coming over on Sunday for lunch and the kids being excited about grandma and wanting to come with Michael to go fetch her . . . safe. It lasted I expect for just a few seconds. But all that time everything was fine . . . just fine.'

I touched her face. She pressed my palm against her cheek and held it there.

'I should take the dress back.'

'That can wait, Rosa.'

'Can it wait?'

'Yes.'

'What if they say I've worn it. What then?'

'I'm sure they won't.'

'Do you like my hair, John?'

'Very much.'

'Should I have had her cut it short?'

'No.'

'Will there come a time when I know what I want again?'

'I'm sure there will.'

'Why aren't I more angry?'

'Shock. I don't . . .'

'He deserved somebody better.'

'You're blaming yourself now. You shouldn't.'

'Am I? Is that what I'm doing?'

'That's what it feels like.'

'OK. Would it be wrong of me to order another drink?'

'You have whatever you want, Rosa.'

The owner sees my half-raised hand, finishes the line in the article he is reading, then slowly slides down from his stool – lifts his eyebrows so he doesn't even have to ask what we want – I tell him one more Scotch, one more vodka. Three drinks each, softening the corners of the day. Already it's too late for anything else, the day has been given over to alcohol. Like Michael said, consciousness is a highly over-rated condition.

This time Rosa sips the vodka, wrinkling her nose to see if she can sniff out the odour of it.

'You're sure about the dress?'

'Forget the dress.'

'Yes . . . fine for you to say that, John. I'm sure your concerns are over loftier things.'

'No. I'm sorry. I don't mean to demean you.'

'But you do. Did. Will always demean me, and, for all I know, the rest of the world. You and Susan. Well . . . just you, now. The great demeaner.'

I shrugged.

'And what it does. When you do this thing to people . . .'

'Look, Rosa . . .'

'No. Hear me out. When you do this thing to people: look at them the way you're looking at me now, you make them, make me feel naked and disgusted with myself. Because that's what demeaners are for. To remind us to be disgusted about ourselves every once in a while . . . What interests me, however, is what happens when two people of this . . . persuasion come together. I mean do you take it in turns or do you just spend all day looking down your pretty noses at each other . . . which one do you do?'

The owner heard all this. The volume at which Rosa was now talking it was impossible for him not to. I saw him pinch the corner of the large front page of his newspaper, lift it, and pull the paper closed.

I said, 'There are no demeaners. Only the demeaned. The demeaned always see people staring at them wherever they are.'

'See?' Rosa turned to the barman. 'And now he's denying it.' She laughed across the rim of her glass. The barman stayed out of it. 'Cowards,' she said, not laughing now, and I felt that both of us had hurt her.

I woke before Rosa. She was breathing deeply, swaddled in the sheets. Michael's wallet was on the table by the bed. Our clothes were folded adultly on the two chairs. The hotel faced onto a small square of grass. An old man was sitting on a wooden bench feeding the birds with crumbs from a bag. As I watched him I thought that we all live on crumbs scattered by somebody.

21. The Gold Room

CLIMBING THE STAIRS of the agency I knew something was wrong. It was the day after Jordan and I got back from Yellowstone. Too quiet: no phones ringing. The stairway was cold and the lino hadn't been swept. Clumps of grey dust had gathered in the back corners of the treads. I pushed open the door. Nobody at the desk. Angel's office empty. No sign of Chester. Just the tap, tap, tap of somebody at a keyboard. I looked round the pillar: Ottie in casuals – jeans and a Nike sweatshirt.

'What's going on?' I said, sitting at my desk. Somebody had used it to pile the mail on.

'Angel has had a stroke.' She looked at me then went on typing.

'Is he OK?'

'He is eighty years old. I expect it will take him some time to recover.'

'A stroke?'

'Yes.'

'So . . .' I looked round the room.

'The agency has been closed. The little business we had, we lost when people heard about Angel.'

'In three weeks?'

'It took two.'

'Two? How come?'

'Angel issued his instructions through his lawyer. He passed on the big accounts. We are not supposed to be allowed on the premises but I took the key.'

'Closed?'

'Get used to it.'

Ottie flouted the smoking ban and lit a cigarette: probably the only one being smoked in any office in Manhattan at that moment in time. She threw her packet over and I took one. Suddenly it felt like the last day of school. Angel had had a stroke: why didn't this mean anything?

'Have you seen him?' I said.

'Nobody from here has seen him.' She was typing like a hack now, cigarette clamped into her mouth, squinting through the smoke. 'His lawyer arrived with an envelope for each of us. He told us we had three hours to collect our belongings before he secured the property. He also thanked us, on behalf of Angel, for our continued and loyal support. Your envelope is in your desk drawer. How he expected you were going to get in and find it I don't know.'

I pulled open the drawer and took out the long brown envelope. Inside was a cheque for fifty thousand dollars and a letter explaining the interim insurance cover. It said that the agency would continue to pay for our healthcare for twelve months or until we were taken on somewhere else, whichever came first.

'I got ten thousand,' Ottie said. 'Which I consider generous. Fifty thousand I think is a little mean.'

'You looked?'

'Of course I looked.'

'What happened? Do you know?'

'The lawyer said he was in bed and the maid found him.

183

He's got some paralysis but he can talk so I suppose we should be thankful for that.'

'You never liked him, did you?'

'He was a bully. If anyone deserved to have a stroke, he did.'

I went into Angel's office and sat in his leather swivel chair. In his desk drawer I found the remote for the TV and a box of Cuban cigars. Under the box was the phone book. I took the book out and found the page with the number of the Hudson Street restaurant. I had spent twelve years with Angel and many evenings eating with him. The telephone number was my key to those evenings and the room flooded with the smell of Chinese food.

Angel's drinks cabinet was fully stocked. I opened a bottle of Jack Daniels and poured two glasses. I took one out to Ottie.

'Thank you but 10.15 in the morning is a little early for me.'

I poured hers into mine and sat in Chester's seat. His desk was clear. 'What's Chester doing?'

'I don't know. We didn't exchange numbers.'

'So what will you do?'

'I'm trying for my old company. I called them and they said I should send in my CV, which I found a little insulting. However, I know how they work. Their feigned indifference is easier to take than their feigned enthusiasm. I spoke to my old boss, he pretended not to remember me.'

'Perhaps he didn't.'

'He did. We live together.'

'Currently?'

'Yes. Currently. He has a peculiar sense of humour, but then, he is Dutch.'

'So you're sending in your CV . . . ?'

'To him, yes.'

I went back into Angel's room and looked through the papers on his desk. The filing cabinet was locked. Ottie called, 'The key is in the bottom desk drawer in the silver cigarette case.'

'Anything worth looking at?'

'Some personal correspondence, some pornography. Some private photographs.' She'd come to the door and was leaning against the frame. I heard her CV printing out in the office.

'Finished?'

'Yes.'

The deep top drawer slid open on oiled bearings. Angel's filing system was neat, and predictably alphabetically ordered.

Ottie said, 'I have removed the incriminating photographs. Should you come across any I'd appreciate it if you destroyed them.'

'Photographs of you?'

'And others.'

'Yes?'

I pulled out a sheaf of invoices: nothing surprising. Neatly printed on each one was the date each was settled and, where applicable, the cheque number.

'What are you looking for?' Ottie said, watching me, curious.

'Answers.'

'To what?'

'Questions.'

'Such as?'

I pushed the drawer shut. 'I don't know.'

She said, 'I found some photographs of Angel's parties.'

'And what did you do with them?'

'I took them home.'

'For the Dutchman?'

'No. He would not understand.'

'Right.'

She came further into the room and sat on the desk. 'So what will you do?'

'I don't know.'

'I could ask my boyfriend if he has anything for you.'

'Yes?'

'Of course.'

'You're a good person, Ottie.'

'I'm not . . . John?'

'Yes.'

'I went to see Michael.'

'And how is he?'

'I think he is a little surprised that you haven't visited him.'

'I get claustrophobic. I don't like to be locked in.'

'He's very sedated.'

'Who isn't?'

'He continues to protest his innocence.'

'Who doesn't?'

'Tell me who did it. I promise I won't tell.'

I sat in Angel's leather chair and swivelled. 'I did.'

Ottie didn't say anything: those TV eyes did the interrogation.

I said, 'Say something.'

'You wouldn't say it if you had.'

'Or maybe that's just what I'd say. Perhaps I need somebody to confide in.'

Ottie sat in my lap. Unexpected, but not unpleasant. She rested her head against my chest. Her perfume smelt of cherries.

'Confide in me.'

I stroked her hair the way I used to stroke Jordan's.

'All right. But it may take some time.'

'I have no other plans for this month.'

★

I took Ottie to England. We stayed for a week at the Cotswold Hotel. We ate lemon chicken. Ottie slept pillowed on my chest. I breathed the aroma of her hair. Sometimes we walked all day, sometimes we hired a car. It rained all the time. Ottie was incurious about the things I thought she'd find interesting. London, which she hadn't visited before, she dismissed with contempt. Nothing big enough or fast enough. New or, indeed, old enough for her. But sometimes she'd stop – once on a stone bridge in the Yorkshire Dales – and when she did she could stand for anything up to an hour just contemplating the scene. On the small bridge (barely a beast's width wide) she craned her neck to look at the clear stream running over the brown pebbles. She pulled out her camera, set the telephoto lens and, leaning down, fired off three rolls of film. When we came to a town she took it into a chemist to be developed. The man said it would take three hours. We waited. She pinned the photographs up on the bedroom wall of the hotel: neatly, edge-to-edge, making the wall look like it had been constructed of pebbles. Ottie stared at it all evening.

When she called the Dutchman I allowed her some privacy and went down to the bar. When I called Jordan at Susan's father's, she sat on the bed and watched me. I don't know what she told her boyfriend, but he didn't seem to mind she was taking a three-week trip with a man she barely knew. A man whose wife had been murdered. And each night she'd listen to the confession. The same story told time after time, again and again. Like a child needing to hear 'The Elves and the Shoemaker'.

'Tell it,' she'd say.

'Not tonight.'

'Please.'

'OK.' And I'd begin. 'Once upon a time there was a king who lived in a castle.'

'Slower.'

'And this king had a daughter who he loved very much. So much so that he wanted her to have everything. The king was a wise man and he knew his daughter had to make her own choices. One day she came home with a shepherd who she'd met when she was riding outside the castle gates. She told the king that she loved this boy and the shepherd loved her too. Well, the old man was unsure about this, but he didn't want to stand in his daughter's way so he said to the shepherd that he could marry the princess and he would provide a dowry. After the wedding the king, who was as good as his word, took the shepherd to a cellar deep in the castle. They stood in a dark corridor facing three doors. The king told him that behind one of these doors was his dowry. Three rooms. One of the rooms was full of gold: unimagined riches. One of the rooms was half full of gold and the other was empty. The shepherd could make his choice. Well, the boy was excited at the prospect of all this wealth and he walked up and down the corridor knocking on the doors as if, in some way, he could ascertain how full the rooms were. But the king stopped him. He said, "If, after a year, you decide you've made the wrong choice, then you can come back, return what you have already taken, and open one more door." Of course, the shepherd couldn't believe his luck. Excited, he stood in front of the middle door and turned the key. Inside, the gold was stacked against the wall: coins, goblets, plates, candlesticks . . . The shepherd embraced his father-in-law and said, "You have made me the richest man on earth." He'd picked the room half full of gold. Then the king said, "One final thing. Should you choose to come back and open another door then you have to give up my daughter and return her to me." The shepherd was puzzled. Why should he want to do that? He had a beautiful bride, he was rich, he had everything a man could want. So he left the castle with the gold and, with the king's daughter, built a great castle far away. Months passed. The shepherd and the princess were happy, but the shepherd couldn't quite forget the choice the king had offered him. He was rich enough never to have to work again, his wife was loyal and loving and beautiful, but at the back of his mind was the prospect of having more. He became withdrawn. He'd take a horse and ride for miles. Sometimes he'd ride as far as the king's castle and look at it from a distance, imagining which of the other two rooms contained the gold and which one was empty. On the eleventh day of the eleventh month the shepherd told his wife what the king had offered him. The princess, knowing her father well, was not surprised. But, being her father's daughter, she did not try to influence the shepherd's decision because she knew that her father had also, in his own way, given her a valuable dowry. The shepherd became more and more unhappy. A week passed. Then another. And finally the shepherd, shamefaced, confronted his bride and, tearfully, told her that he could not live the rest of his life with her not knowing whether he would have chosen the room that was full of gold. So they left the castle they had built together, collected what remained of the gold, and rode back to the king. The old man met them at the gate. He was sad. He told them he'd become convinced that the shepherd had learned to live with his choice, but he could understand why he needed to return. He left his daughter and the man to say goodbye. They kissed, and parted, and the girl passed through the door in the castle gates. The shepherd stood, waiting for the gates to swing open so he could go down into the basement with the king and open another door.'

When I told this story to Ottie the first time she said, 'This is a confession?'

'Yes.'

'Your confession?'

When I told this story to Ottie a second time she said, 'It is so typical that the woman in this story is at the mercy of the men. She has no free will. Everything is decided for her.'

'It's a fairy story.'

'But what does it mean? That we are always defeated by choice?'

'It means what you want it to mean.'

'Sometimes you tire me, John.'

I tried to call Ray and tell the story to him, but he never got back to me.

I called Rosa to tell her the story but her ansaphone was on so I told it to her machine. She wrote to me and called me a bastard, saying how insensitive I'd been. She said she didn't want me to contact her again.

When I told this story to Jordan he didn't say anything straight away. When he did, it was: 'The shepherd would always have made that choice. Whoever he was.'

I said, surprising myself, 'And Mom?'

'She did. She made that choice.'

'And do you blame her?'

Jordan turned away. The TV always made greater claims on his attention than anything I could say to him.

'Do you?' I said. Jordan has Susan's profile. I watched it for a while as he decided how to answer.

'I did blame her,' he said. 'But for you.'

'What do you mean?'

'I blamed her for you. That's what I mean.'

'You stood up for me?'

'Kind of.'

22. Delores Zane

WHEN I TOLD the story to Angel, he said, 'All the rooms were half full of gold, yes?'

I said, 'Could be.'

His laugh was a rasp. 'You always wanted to have it every way you could, John.'

We were in a white room in a silent white hospital. Angel seemed to be the only patient there. A different nurse came in every five minutes to check on his progress. Each one managed to voice concern in a novel way. Most of them were young women. Since the stroke the folds in Angel's face looked deeper. Around his eyes, the blue had become black, more black because his nightshirt was an incredible white. The muscles on the right side of his face were frozen. When I leaned down to embrace him he reached to wipe some saliva off his chin and said, 'See? Half dead already. I'm doing it on the instalment plan.'

I sat beside the bed on a leather chair and asked him how he was. He said what little time he had left he didn't want to waste answering stupid questions. When I thanked him for the fifty thousand dollars he said, 'Tear it up . . . Don't look like that at me. Tear it up.'

'I cashed it.'

'Take a look in that drawer over there.'

I opened the drawer in his dresser. Inside were a number of envelopes. One of them had my name on it. 'Find it?'

'Yes.'

'Open it.'

I slit it open. A cheque for five hundred thousand dollars. I said, 'I don't understand.'

'That German bitch let you in to the agency?'

'Ottie was there, yes.'

'Right, she stole a key. And she opened your envelope. Take my word for it. She tries to cash her cheque, it bounces. You fuck her?'

'None of your business, Angel.'

'OK. So you did. And I'm guessing you did it after she looked in your envelope and not before. Did she not inform you her cheque bounced?'

'I never asked.'

'You spend some money on her?'

'What do you expect me to do with this money?'

'Exercise a few choices.' He closed his eyes. I thought he'd gone to sleep, but he was just thinking.

'It's too much.'

'No such prospect. I live another six months you'll be back for more. Believe me. The more you have the easier it gets to spend. Was there some time in your life when you didn't spend every dollar you earned?'

'Well . . .'

'The same principle applies however rich you are. Home here, home there. Charter a yacht round the Caribbean? Sure. Why charter? Why not buy one? Good investment, my accountants say. Good investment my ass. You employ a woman to try to get this yacht chartered out when you're not using it, except nobody wants it. You know why? Because the people who can afford it just bought their own yacht and all the yachts are anchored together in some blue lagoon. Captains playing cards, spending my money on diesel and food, *fucking* the women, fucking each other for all I know. And all the time I'm here and worrying about how I'm going to spend my next hundred thousand dollars. Buy yourself a yacht. No. This is what you do. You buy yourself a yacht, you don't get round to insuring it. You sink it. Your money is spent. This is what you should do.'

'I don't need a yacht.'

'Buy Jordan a yacht.'

Another nurse comes in. The uniform is powder-blue, trousers and smock made of something that looks like paper. Throwaway slip-on overshoes. The woman is Filipino. Angel brightens. 'Ask her name.' This to me.

'What?'

'Ask the nurse her name.'

I turn to the nurse, embarrassed, and say, 'He wants to know your name.'

The nurse giggles, plumps up Angel's pillows and leaves.

'I like to hear her laugh,' Angel said. 'I try to get her to give me a little manual relief but she pretends she doesn't understand. I say, the amount I'm paying for this bed you'd better go and get yourself some lessons in speakin' da English, baby. Then she says she doesn't understand why a handsome man like me needs to ask a nurse to help me out. This is why I don't mind paying two hundred dollars an hour for this fucking funeral-parlour-in-waiting. Intelligence. Intelligent lies. Good psychology.' He turned away so I couldn't see his face. 'Turn on the TV. Don't stare at me.'

I switched it on. Then I heard, 'Stop calling the detective.'

'What?'

'Leave it alone. It's finished.'

A man spun a horizontal wheel. An old-fashioned

gameshow with an old-fashioned host in a glossy suit who looked like an insurance salesman.

'Are you saying what I think you're saying?'

Angel said, 'You know what costs the most? Freedom is the most expensive commodity around.' He tries to sit up but he doesn't seem to have the strength. I stand and offer him my arm to lean on. He takes it, then settles back exhausted against his pillows. 'Listen to this. Twenty, twenty-five years ago this woman calls me and tells me I knocked her up. Nice woman, sounded educated. She wasn't trying to shake me down or anything like that. She tells me where we met. I don't remember her. She needs money for the child, that's all. We have a reasonable conversation. Two reasonable adults conversing. If she telephoned and threatened maybe I'd deal with it another way. But we're reasonable. So I ask her, how much do you want? The woman says ten thousand dollars should see her through the worst. I send her thirty thousand with the proviso that she lets me know when the baby is born. We congratulate each other again on how very reasonable we are being. A few months later I get a card through the post. The announcement of the birth of a son to Delores Zane or whatever her name is. I throw the card away but I go round all day being very nice to people. You know, strutting around, carnation in my lapel, feeling good about the world . . . This lasts for a week and I think about Delores Zane and I think about the boy and then I forget them both. Twenty-five years later Leona is murdered.'

'Susan?'

'You remember you called me up?'

'Yes.'

A trolley glides past the door on silent castors, the shrill squeak of rubber on lino from the shoes of the porter. Slow motion.

'You know the first thing I thought?'

'No.'

'I thought, I wonder whatever happened to Delores Zane?'

Moments of significance have their own special weight. Time stops. You become aware of your heart beating.

'Go on.'

'A son needs his father.' Angel looks at me, pressing the meaning on me. 'Women can look after themselves.'

'Michael's daughters?'

'Women can look after themselves.'

'Rosa?'

'Like I said. Freedom is expensive. You pay for lawyers, you pay for judges in certain ways. You offer to pay for the upkeep of certain loved ones should the court result not fall in your favour. You point out there is, in the present jargon, collateral damage that you would rather avoid if you get my meaning. And for this you ask something in return.'

'You offered to support Rosa if Michael didn't mention Gramercy Park?'

'That's a very direct way of stating what was a somewhat complex transaction.'

'And Ray. You're not telling me you paid him?'

'Just accept some advice from a dying man. Leave it alone. Acknowledge that Michael Conway was no way going to walk out of the courtroom a free man. Absolve yourself of any further guilt.'

'You thought I killed Susan?'

'The fuck does it matter what I thought? I could see how it might be construed that you might just have shot her. Are you angry?'

'Yes.'

'You should be. Feel like you've just been banged up the ass by an old Jew? You have been. So don't make me angry.

195

Don't call the detective. He does not need to be troubled by your liberal conscience. He has one of his own. You two get together you might just cause enough problems to make somebody take another look at the case.'

I hear the man at the switchboard and wonder now if my messages have been passed to Ray.

'Then I have this stroke. This woman is sitting on my face. Next thing is I can't move my jaw and my arm feels like somebody tied it to my side. Tubes coming out of me. I get them to call up my lawyer. It's night so they get him out of bed. The doctors tell me I need to rest. I say why rest? Soon I'm getting all the rest I need. So my lawyer, Jerry, comes in. His tie is a little loose. I tell him, "Jerry, it's 3 a.m. but I don't pay this kind of money for a lawyer who can't tie his tie." I give him a list of instructions. 'A few hundred for the woman who was riding me when it happened. Settle up the agency accounts. Make sure you draw the cheque for that German bitch on a closed account, and find Delores Zane. Find her. Find my son. "If there's only one thing you do in your life from now on, Jerry, make it this." I should have started this when Leona got shot. That's when I should have got Jerry onto it. Except I didn't know it then. Do you understand, John? It's only by looking back that you recognise the first clue. Like the pain you get in your arm two weeks before your coronary.'

'And did he find him?'

Angel shifts against his pillows and the pain registers on his face. 'Yeah. Thin kid. Twenty-three years old. Ugly. Christ only knows what Delores looks like. He teaches guitar to schoolkids. He wants to be in a rock and roll band. Looks like Buddy Holly. Blind in one eye. Something wrong with one of his legs. My son the half-blind cripple. Jerry brings him in a limousine. I told him to hire a big black limousine for the occasion. Not to tell the boy anything, nice surprise. I get champagne on ice brought in here. Kid thinks he's been busted by the FBI. He should be that interesting. Then he starts wondering if it's some *X-Files* conspiracy. Stands by my bed and asks if I'm the cancer man. The boy is an idiot. He's carrying his guitar in a case. I tell him to get it out and play me something. Takes forever trying to tune it up. Breaks a string. Still doesn't sound right. It doesn't matter, I tell him, I'm dying and I don't want to spend what remains of my life listening to a gimp tuning a guitar. He puts the guitar on his knee and sings me a song. His voice sounds like Slim Whitman, all yodelee. The song concerns a fucking oak tree. Rhymes it with eternity. Brings tears to my eyes. I tell Jerry to take him home. Give him ten dollars for some new guitar strings. Make sure the kid doesn't find out I'm his father. I don't want any claims on my estate . . . I expect he gets home and tells Delores he's been abducted by aliens. Looks like I chose the empty room, doesn't it?'

'Goodbye Angel.' I stand and stretch. Seeing somebody in pain always makes me tense up, as though I'm anticipating feeling the pain myself. Outside, sprinklers are watering the lush lawn.

Angel's exhausted now. He says, 'One thing the story reminded me of.'

'Yes?'

'Do you remember George Gribbin's favourite piece of copy?'

'No.' I move to the door. I'm carrying the cheque.

'No headline. This is his piece for Travellers Insurance. Goes something like this. He's written it from the point of view of a woman.' His voice is fading now. He looks up at the harsh lights on the ceiling and remembers. 'Goes something like: "When I was twenty-eight, I thought I'd probably never get married. I'd always been over-tall and my hands and feet were always getting in my way. Also my

clothes never look nice on me like other girls . . ."
Remember it now, John?'

'Yes.'

' "It seemed certain that no knight would ever come along
on his big white horse and carry me away. But a man did
come along. Everett wasn't the masterful type you dream
about when you're young. He was a shy and awkward fellow
who didn't know what to do with his hands and his feet. He
saw something in me that I didn't know I had myself. I
actually began to feel like somebody . . . both of us did . . ." '

But Angel can't sustain it. He's tired so I offer to excuse
myself. I stop at the door. I know I'll never see him alive
again. He's looking at me because he knows it too. There's
twenty or so feet between us and all I have to do is to cross it
and embrace him and say goodbye. What stops me from
doing so is thinking about Michael Conway. I wave instead,
standing on the quay, bidding farewell to somebody who's
about to set sail away from the world.

When I get home I call up Ottie and ask her to meet me at
the agency with the key. We look round Angel's office for
the Gribbin copy and I find it in the filing cabinet under
Gribbin. Angel had remembered it almost word for word. I
read the rest of it out to Ottie as she smoked:

' "Pretty soon, we got so used to each other that we felt
loose when we weren't together, so we figured it probably
was the sort of love you read about in the story books, and
we got married. It was a day in April. And the apple trees
were in blossom, and the whole earth smelt sweet. That was
nearly thirty years ago and it's been that way almost every
day since. I can't believe so many years have gone by. They
just carried Ev and me along so peacefully, like a canoe on a
quiet river, that you didn't realise you were moving . . . We
never went to Europe. We never even went to California. I
guess we didn't need to, for home was big enough for us. I

wish we'd had children. But we couldn't. I was like Sarah in the bible, only the Good Lord didn't work a miracle for me. Perhaps He thought Everett was enough ... Well, Ev died two years ago last April. Quietly and smilingly, just as he had lived. The apple trees were in blossom and the earth again smelt sweet. I felt too numb to cry. When my brother came to help me straighten out Ev's affairs, I found he'd been thoughtful, as I suppose men built like him always are. There wasn't a great deal in the bank, but there was an insurance policy that will take care of all my needs as long as I live. I'm as content as a woman can be when a man she really loved has gone ... And the moral: Insure in The Travelers Insurance Company, Hartford, Connecticut." '

I'm lying with Ottie that night in bed and we're talking. The pillowcase smells like cherry blossom, Jordan has just looked round the door and said goodnight. He's carrying a tall glass of milk balanced on a hardback book Ottie bought him: *Out of the Dark Headfirst*. It's the latest and last of the *Quom Bandit* series and chronicles the final years of Herb Todd, water miner. According to Jordan, Herb, an old man now, is down on his luck and he's working as a travelling salesman, going from galaxy to galaxy in his trusty ship. He cold-calls distant planets and tries to sell them encyclopaedias. Many of these new planets have been colonised by those who had to leave earth when the water ran out (Herb's scheme to bring the permafrost back from Mars failed – Lorna never solved the re-entry problem and the frost melted). When Herb arrives and puts his foot in the airlock, he doesn't say, 'Can I interest you in an encyclopaedia?', he says, 'What do you know about your history?' Usually he's greeted with blank stares: these Lost in Space kids left in a hurry, many of them didn't even tell their parents they were going. They say to him history is what happened five minutes ago, what happened before that is irrelevant. So Herb says, 'OK, say somebody was dying and one of you came up with a cure and that person lived. Then, years later, somebody else came down with the same disease, but the person who'd discovered the cure was dead. Wouldn't it be useful to write it all down so that those who come after you can learn from your experiences?' The people say, 'So that's history, is it?' And he says, 'Yes, history is lessons somebody else took the trouble of learning for you, and what's more I have two or three thousand years' worth of them written down in these twenty-four leatherbound volumes.' So they reach into their pockets and they pay. It's only when Herb blasts off and they open the books do they find that he's left them with the 1964 edition. This is how far Jordan has got, so the implications have yet to be revealed.

'Goodnight,' Jordan says politely to the girl in his father's bed. He won't come through the door and into the room, but he will talk to us from the doorway.

'Sleep tight.'

Ottie waves to him like a backstroke swimmer heading away from the shore.

We go back to our conversation. 'Yes,' I say, 'I have this peculiar belief that there will be some kind of reunion. Otherwise it all means nothing.'

'A reunion of who? Everybody you've ever known?'

'No. A school reunion. Because that's who you measure yourself against. I think I'd feel cheated if I never went to a school reunion and found out what everybody was doing.'

'Is this because of me?' Ottie said.

'No. Of course not,' I said, then I realised it was. What did I have to show but Ottie and Jordan, a cheque for five hundred thousand dollars. Forty-six thousand dollars left of the other cheque, a rent-controlled apartment, no job and . . . what?

'Tell me again,' Ottie says sleepily, 'this boy was collected in a black limousine?'

'So Angel said.'

'From where?'

'I don't know.'

'And when did this happen?'

'Last week sometime.'

'Mm.'

The next morning I wake up to find Ottie gone and the phonebook out on the table. It's covered in flakes from her croissant. The book is open at the executive car hire page. Ottie is looking for the key to Angel's wealth. A half-blind boy who teaches guitar to schoolchildren. What chance will he stand against her single-mindedness? What hurts most is how Jordan is going to take it. He liked Ottie and he'll blame me for her leaving.

23. Angel Swings

Susan once told me that when Andy Warhol painted he played one record over and over again: 'Sally Goes Round the Roses' by the Jaynetts. The accompaniment to my life now is the sound of closing doors. I don't like change but lately it seems that change is the only constant.

Chester phoned and told me that Angel was dead. He found this out when he called Jerry to tell him he'd got a new job and he wanted to check out his pension and insurance situation vis-à-vis the agency. Jerry told him that Angel had been buried in a small private ceremony. Only three people were invited, Jerry wasn't one of them. Chester asked me what I made of it and I told him it would take some time for it to sink in. He was calling on a mobile and said he was eating with a friend. They were waiting for the first course and the friend had just gone to the lavatory. That's where I stand now in Chester's estimation – an aperitif.

'It struck me a few weeks ago,' I told him, 'just why you came round after Susan died.'

'Listen, John, I really have to . . .'

'Angel told you to. You were spying on me.'

'It wasn't just that.'

'But that was part of it?'

'Look. It was for your own . . .'

'I thought you were a friend.'

'Yeah. I know.'

Susan, Carol, Michael, Angel, Ottie, Angela, Ray, Carl
and now Chester. Slam, slam, slam.

'This is your lake of poisoned humanity, Chester?'

Chester, now I think regretting making this call in a public
place, went on the offensive. 'What do you want me to say?
Because whatever I say to you will never be enough.
Nothing anybody says to you, John, is ever enough.'

'I . . .'

'You're a very needy person, but I did respect you. I wish
I could say I liked you but . . . excuse me.' His friend arrived
back from the lavatory. The background noise on the line
cut as Chester covered the mouthpiece.

'Back,' he said.

'You were saying, you wished you could say you liked
me, but . . . ?'

'Not now. How's Ottie?'

'Who knows.'

'Jerry said Angel was with her when he had his stroke. Is
that right?'

'Jesus.'

'Amen to that. Got to go. Here comes the pasta.'

Trying to imagine Angel's parties is like trying to imagine
Heaven or Hell. You can populate them whichever way you
like to make them real for you – and every day you do it in a
different way. Sometimes I glimpse the stairway of the
Gramercy Park house: it's after midnight, halfway through
the weekend. People, naked, in masks, hanging over the
banisters looking down at the carnage of bodies beneath
them. A heaving sea of bodies. A naked woman on a white
horse. A fountain of red wine. A woman being fed red grapes

by a beautiful golden-haired boy, her hand tugging away beneath his toga. Stairs down to the dark basement rooms where the rest of it goes on. A woman on a table taking it both ways. A circle watching, both men and women, but they're holding each other too: hands round waists, cupping breasts, cupping anything. A trapeze strung high from a chandelier with a naked adolescent girl riding it: laughing and spraying everybody with a shower of champagne. The girl is Heaven, or innocence, swinging there because when people look up from the floor they see her and feel ashamed. Only because she is beautiful and laughing she seems to condone what they're doing and they don't feel so sad. Lust is the gravity that keeps us down in the gutter. Love is what makes us raise our head to look at the stars. Oscar Wilde only got it half right. He never ascribed a motive. Angel once said to me that man is born of a woman's womb and spends the rest of his life trying to climb back in there. They should put that on his gravestone. I hope he's happy now, swinging with his new congregation.

Thinking about Hell reminds me that Eva Something, the grief facilitator, destroyed me for a couple of months. Not long after her late-night visit (the one at which she empathised and made me coffee and cleared the garbage from the pail in the kitchen), a dour man and a woman arrived at the apartment: she was wearing a blue rain mac, he a brown suit. I asked them to come in, talking to them all the time, offering them coffee or something to drink. In short, being very polite, and thinking what nice people they were to be showing such concern. I got a sense that while the man quite liked me, the woman didn't. They were interested in Jordan, and they seemed to know a good deal about him. The woman, who wouldn't take her coat off, asked whether I was aware he was cutting school. She was wearing black stockings, which I found unsettling because her tweed skirt was quite short. Good legs, too. She kept squirming around on the sofa, pulling her hem down as far as it would go. I must have been making her feel uncomfortable. The man didn't seem to be aware of it. He had the cool distance of a Jehovah's witness. You could never imagine this neat man with his razor-sharp side parting ever harbouring urges – natural or otherwise.

When I told the woman that I wasn't aware that Jordan was cutting school, this provoked a meaningful look between the two of them and the man jotting something down onto a pad which he'd pulled out of his briefcase. (On the strap, gold lettering: L.H.R.) I also said that if he was then I wasn't surprised because, although I wouldn't go so far as to condone it, Jordan had been through a lot recently and he needed to find his own way to deal with it.

'He attacked a boy. Were you aware of that?' the Mac asked.

'No, I was not aware of that. Would you like to explain to me just who you are and what you're doing here.'

'We're here to assess the situation,' the Suit said.

'In what respect?'

'Would you like to talk us through your routine, please.' The Suit poised his pen.

'Is this absolutely necessary?'

'Absolutely.'

'OK . . . my daily routine?'

'If that's what you choose.'

'Is there some other routine you're interested in?'

The Mac: 'No, there isn't.'

'Then why don't you just say it: tell me about your daily routine. OK?'

He conceded with a nod.

'Fine. My daily routine.' A decision here – the truth or a

lie. What the hell, they'd probably cross-examine me anyway and find me out. 'OK. I get up at around 9 a.m.'

The Suit said, 'And by this time Jordan has already left for school?'

'Yes. I expect so ... most days he's already gone. Sometimes he lies in and I have to wake him, but most of the time when I get up he's gone.'

The Suit smiled encouragement. 'Good. That's fine.'

'Then I make a cup of coffee, if Jordan has not made me one and left it in the microwave. I have to open the microwave to check. Lately, however, Jordan has been leaving open the door of the microwave to remind me because he gets pissed off if he comes home from school and the coffee he's made me is still in there. You see the steam just messes up the inside of the ... is this too much detail?'

They look at each other. I take it as a no.

'OK. So after the coffee which I drink sitting at the table over there, reading the paper if I can find it – any paper, doesn't matter which day, if I can't find a paper I'll read a cereal box or something – I might take a shower. Sometimes I don't. I probably take a shower every other day. In the winter, when the apartment is cold, I take fewer showers than in summer when the apartment is hot. In summer I expect I shower every day, in the winter it's probably every other day. Perhaps twice every three days ...'

Sometimes yesterday is today. The thought came into my head as I talked to them but there was nothing I could do about it. I just had to go on.

'... And when I shower I turn the hot tap on first, full on. Then notch it back about halfway because the little black numerals have worn off so unless you go all the way you can't judge what halfway is. Does that make sense? ... OK, then I turn on the cold, about a quarter turn. And by then the temperature is about right ... so I step under the shower after removing my robe and leaving it draped over the bath. Unless I use the lavatory first. If I do, then I have already removed my robe to achieve that. I probably use the lavatory to move my bowels once – sometimes twice a day. I always look in the pan, and what I see never fails to surprise me. I mean it's the one big surprise we give ourselves each day, wouldn't you say?'

The Suit sighs and puts down his pad.

'After the shower I go back into the kitchen and pour myself a drink. Scotch usually. I have a rule that I do not drink before 10 a.m. and I am very strict about this. So, the first drink, which I bring through into here and sit on the sofa and turn on the television and watch it while I drink . . . sometimes I'm dressed by now, sometimes I'm not. Then I remember about this time to check the sheets. Sometimes I wet the bed so I have to wash the sheets. If I wet the bed then I always have a shower – winter or summer. Did you want to say something?'

The Suit shook his head. The Mac said, 'Mr Wayne, if we could concentrate a little on Jordan's role in your routine.'

'Jordan?'

'If you wouldn't mind.'

'You didn't say that.'

'We're asking now.'

'Well . . . I mean, that's a little hard to . . . OK, well Jordan gets back to the house at . . . Jordan gets back at around . . . 5 p.m.? Something like that, and he . . . I mean we . . . more usually he . . .'

The Mac cut in: 'It has been reported to us that Jordan is left to fend for himself.'

'Is that a crime?'

'Of course it isn't a crime, Mr Wayne.'

'Good. Only I thought you were going to arrest me for leaving my son to fend for himself.'

The Suit: 'We don't have the authority to arrest people.'

The Mac: 'What are your meal arrangements?'

'Well, we like to order in some pizza some days. Yes, some days we do that . . .'

'But generally?' The Suit was casting round the room for something to look at. He already seemed to have made up his mind about whatever it was he'd come to see me about.

'Generally? Well, generally . . . can I get you a coffee or something?'

'That would be very nice,' the Mac said, and followed me into the kitchen. I was aware of the Suit going somewhere else. 'Don't mind my colleague, his curiosity is insatiable.'

'So who . . . I mean, you haven't really told me . . .' I was playing for time. I couldn't find the coffee. There were some flies in the kitchen and the pail was full again. 'Did you say who you were working for?'

'We're employed by the ACS.'

'Yes? The ACS?' No coffee in the wall cupboard either.

'The Administration for Children's Services. We're case workers.'

'And I'm a case?'

'That's what we're here to assess.'

'Look . . .' I poured three Scotches. That was all I could find. The woman took her glass and held it at arm's length. 'Tell me about Jordan.'

'Jordan fought with another boy last week. The other child was quite badly hurt. His parents made a complaint to the school.'

'All children fight.'

'Yes, of course,' she soothed.

We were back by the sofa. The Mac sat down and put her glass on the table. The Suit walked in and coughed to get her attention. I offered him his Scotch but he didn't take it.

Instead, he beckoned the Mac and she followed him towards Jordan's room. I tagged on behind, curious now because I hadn't been in there for two or three months.

They stood by the door and I stood with them. I have to admit the room was not a pretty sight. Jordan had upturned his bed and shoved it against the wall. He'd been sleeping on a pile of blankets on the floor. Unfortunately the floor was obscured by empty pizza boxes, cans of Coke, slabs of dried-up garlic bread. The kitchen portable TV was in there on a chair. I'd wondered where it had gone. All of Jordan's clothes were on the floor. He'd half-painted one of the walls in purple. The curtains were closed. Something moved under one of the pizza boxes. The Mac said, 'I think we've seen enough.'

When they'd gone I packed a bag for Jordan, washed some of his clothes in the basement washing machines and folded them. Then I bought him a two-litre bottle of Coke, a game for his GameBoy and a new sweatshirt. When he got home from school he looked at me with shock because I was sober. Then he saw the bag on the floor.

'I think you might be going to live somewhere else for a while,' I said.

'I didn't tell them,' Jordan said.

Twelve years old now and an adult. What did we do to him?

He was gone for two months. This was the intense Carol period – before the trip to Cody and Yellowstone where the healing began. When they kidnapped him they tried to do it gently so he didn't get upset. The Mac took him out to the car, explaining where he was going, putting a hand on his shoulder. I called, 'Goodbye, son.'

'Bye . . . Dad.'

The tears did us both good.

The Suit waited with me and explained that, 'Only when

families demonstrate they can provide safe and secure homes will children be permitted to return home.'

'Thanks.'

At the door, he offered, 'When children cannot be returned safely to their homes, they will be provided with alternative safe, loving, permanent homes.' One more look round the room and he was gone.

There was a present for me on the kitchen counter. Jordan had bought me a packet of coffee and wrapped it up. A note tied to it said, 'Back soon.'

I protested when they took Jordan to see a psychiatrist but it seemed I didn't have any say in the matter. I asked Carol whether she thought Steve might pull a few strings to get Jordan back but she just said she thought I'd probably had enough to drink. Six weeks on Jordan's shrink called me and asked me to go and see her. I was glad of the break in the routine. By now I was spending all morning sober and I was looking to extend this through the afternoon. One step at a time. I was making it to work three days a week for anything up to six hours a time.

The woman had a firm handshake and a very healthy smile. 'Call me June,' she said dazzling me with her teeth.

'I will. June.' We both laughed.

June was large and sunny which she said was no surprise because that was why her parents had named her: she was born that month.

'Lucky it wasn't October,' I said.

'I don't know, October has a certain ring to it, don't you think?'

'Sounds like a name for a whale,' I said, by now settled in the chair facing her across her broad desk. Coat across my knee. 'October the whale,' I said, in my best Orson Welles voice.

'I suppose it does,' June said.

'I just meant . . .'

She helped me out. 'No, October is a very good name for a whale.'

'June. I'm not going to be offended if you don't think October is a good name for a whale so don't feel you have to be so reasonable about it.'

'I didn't imagine you were, John.'

'Tuesday Weld,' I said, 'I expect she was born . . . in October.'

June laughed with less conviction, then got down to the business in hand. 'Jordan,' she announced like a chapter heading. 'OK, let me just give you a little of the background here.' She looked at her notes.

'You see I wasn't entirely happy that Jordan was being brought to see you.'

Waving this objection aside, she said, 'No. I know that, but it was considered in his best interests.'

'OK.'

'Jordan is . . . Jordan is a very unhappy child.'

'This is the Jordan whose mother was killed?' I laid my coat down on the floor, my knees were hot.

'I'm sorry?'

'You're suggesting that Jordan is unhappy. Tell me something I don't know.'

'Profoundly unhappy.'

'That doesn't narrow it down a great deal. And saying "profoundly" doesn't add profundity to the statement.'

June had gone cloudy. Rain looked imminent. 'One of his recurring concerns is the guilt he feels over the death of his mother.'

I probed a tooth with my tongue. Short of biting it, it was all I could do.

'Do you have a problem with this, Mr Wayne? Because if

you do it would perhaps be for the best if we called this meeting to a close.'

'I have a problem with being told things I already know. I have a problem with people being paid large sums of money to state some very simple truths. OK, truth is . . .'

She cut in, 'Why are you finding it necessary to perform?'

'What?'

'We're not here for your benefit, Mr Wayne. We're here for Jordan. So can we spend a little time discussing . . .'

'I'm intrigued to know what gives you the right to make that kind of judgement about me.'

'Please, Mr Wayne.'

'You stole my son. I want him back. So fuck you.'

I stood up.

June pressed a buzzer. A man burst into the room dressed in blue janitor's overalls. He was holding a salami sandwich, the meat protruding obscenely from the edge like the tongue of a shoe. He stopped by the desk and stood stock still. The three of us waited in silence. The man looked at me, June looked out of the window. I shrugged apologetically at the janitor, cocking my head at June and raising my eyebrows, trying to win him on to my side by playing the male solidarity ticket. It didn't work. His dim, doleful face registered nothing beyond the panic it had shown when he lurched through the door.

I sat down.

'Thank you, Frank,' June said a minute or so later. The man went out to finish his lunch. 'Can we begin again?'

Jordan, it transpired, had told June that he killed his mother. Not that he felt responsible for it, but that he had actually killed her. He pulled the trigger on the gun and shot her. They couldn't seem to convince him otherwise.

'So what do you make of that?' June asked me.

'You're the shrink.'

'Yes. I know what I think. I was asking what you made of it, Mr Wayne.'

'I once caught Jordan grilling a cockroach, an American cockroach, better get that right. I never really knew what to make of that so you can't expect me to comment on what he's now choosing to construct around the death of his mother.'

'One last time, Mr Wayne. Just tell me what you make of it.'

I said, 'I could not countenance that behaviour.'

June sighed and looked out of the window again. I finally got her to tell me what she thought of Jordan's confession. She said it didn't surprise her. Does anything surprise psychiatrists? I asked her. When I left she said she'd see what she could do about getting them to give Jordan back to me. It was then I realised that Jordan was only the pretext for the meeting. She'd been assessing me.

Just when I thought she was gone for good, Ottie called and told me she'd found Angel's son. It had taken her a week and she was sorry she hadn't let me know what she was doing but the search had consumed her. I never knew what happened to the Dutchman, but after our trip to England Ottie never mentioned his name again and when I called her number, his name was no longer after hers on the witty trilingual machine message. Ottie said she had told Angel's son everything and, with his mother's help, he was now making up his mind what to do next. He was, it seems, a sensitive individual. Ottie's portrait of him clashed with that of Angel's. Angel used to see humanity as weakness. What concerned the boy most was not his father's fortune but whether Angel was musical because his mother wasn't and he thought he must have inherited his gift from one of his parents. He said he

thought he must have been because when he played him
'Oak Tree', Angel cried.

Ottie asked why I was angry at her. I didn't tell her I'd
assumed the worst and that I'd been happy to believe she was
the gold-digging bitch that Angel had painted her. Instead,
I told her that Chester had heard she'd been with Angel the
night he had his stroke. She denied it and asked if I'd
forgotten that Angel used lies to destroy people. Then Ottie
said, 'I've missed you, John.'

'Have you?'

'Yes. It surprises me perhaps as much as it surprises you.'

Which showed just how well she knew me and maybe it
was that, as much as anything, that prompted me to say, 'I
have five hundred thousand dollars in cheque form. I have
nearly fifty thousand dollars in an account. I have a rent-
controlled apartment. I have no employment but I do have a
son who, for much of the time, is quite nice to know. How
would you like to marry me?'

'Would you like to ask that question again and leave out
the unromantic bits.'

'Ottie, I think I'm in love with you. Will you marry me?'

'. . . I don't know.'

'You still think I killed Susan don't you?'

'The man I think I know didn't.'

'That's the man I am.'

'What about the man you were?'

'He's gone.'

'I can't give you an answer now. Give me some time.'

'To make up your mind about whether I killed Susan?'

'I'll tell you in a week.'

'A week, why?'

'I need some time. In a week I'll meet you.'

'OK.'

'Is that fair?'

'Of course.'

'Where?'

'Meet me in Central Park. At the Boathouse Café. Midday.'

'OK, John.'

'You will come?'

'You'll have your answer then, John, I promise.'

24. Newton's Swing – 2

THE MAN AT the garage says that people seem to want air-con nowadays and that, since we took it to Yellowstone, the VW Camper has been out only once. Jordan and I walk past the rows of shiny vehicles to the back of the garage and the green van with the white roof greets us with a smile. I climb in, Jordan gets in the other side and I turn the key with the registration on the small white tag tied to it. With a metallic chuckle, the old engine starts (54876 on the clock – the mechanic says he's unsure whether it's been round once or twice). We edge past the inspection kit, stop at the glassed-in booth by the tall doors to collect the documentation, then bump out of the dark and onto Franklin Street. We're going to the coast for a few days. Time enough to tell Jordan about Ottie, time to walk along the sand together, time to see Henry and Maude, and time to think about whether or not we'll stay on in New York.

Jordan has already called Mrs Lomax and she's started baking. She has this Pavlovian reflex whenever she knows someone is coming to visit her. She also told him that she's going to get the beds aired so that if we arrive late we can go straight up and neither of us will catch a chill. She says she's looking forward to seeing how Jordan has grown in the twelve months since we were last there. Jordan describes the conversation with suitable disparagement, but I know he's excited about the trip. Wherever you visit when you're a child, you leave something of yourself behind. When you go back, however much time has passed, you can always retrieve a little of it.

No tent this time. No cots or tin pans. Just two bags which, quite proudly, we've packed and put next to each other by the apartment door. There's a fight going on as to who has folded his clothes the most efficiently. When he was away, Jordan was taught to fold his shirts inside out and he demonstrates this method to me. What he did during these two months emerges this way: in a trickle of practical information, as though he'd gone to college to learn how to be a model child. I decide to settle for the tried and tested sleeves crossed over the front, one half fold left over right, then top to bottom, then into the bag. Two pairs of denims bundled on top, a pile of underwear and socks and two handkerchiefs. Jordan has bought three books to read: Tolkien, Kurt Vonnegut and a writer whose name I don't know. I also load in a carrier bag which contains just one bottle of Johnny Walker Black Label. I have had this bottle for a month and it remains unopened.

We swing onto Route 95 just after seven. The headlights process along the road for miles ahead, evenly spaced; up and over a long gentle incline. Jordan has his feet up on the dash and he's reading his book with a torch. It seems like as good a time as any to tell him about Ottie. If he freaks, we can turn round and go home. But how to start? I clear my throat. Jordan infers a respiratory blockage, reaches down for the bottled water, unscrews the top and passes it over. I take a draught, then pass it back.

'Thanks.'

Jordan drops it into the well at his feet.

'Jordan?'

'Yup.' He turns a page and goes on reading.

'Jordan?'

He looks over at me. 'What?'

'I want to tell you something.'

Wary, he switches off his torch and waits. A lorry zooms close in the rear-view mirror then backs off.

'This is . . . look. You know Ottie?'

'No.'

'I'm trying to be serious.'

'Yes, Dad, I know Ottie.'

'Well, you know we've been seeing a lot of each other . . .'

'You've seen each other naked?' Jordan chortled.

'If you're not going to take this seriously then . . .'

'OK.' Jordan zips his lips.

'I've asked Ottie to marry me.'

'Why?'

'Because, because I like her. She makes me happy . . . I like spending time with her.'

'OK.'

Jordan switches on his torch again and opens his book. He doesn't turn a page for ten miles. Then he says, 'And what about me?'

'You?'

'When you get married. Do I go live with gramps?'

'No. You'll live with us.'

'Won't Ottie mind?'

'Do you think I'd marry somebody who didn't love you like I did?'

'You might.'

'Of course I wouldn't.'

'OK . . . do I have to wear a tie at the wedding?'

'Not if you don't want to.'

'Good.'

'She hasn't said yes yet.'

'When will we know?'

Mrs Lomax is waiting for us on the porch when we arrive. It's 11.15 and few of the other houses in the street are lit. Jordan, despite himself, runs up to her and she embraces him then pushes him away to look at him, then pulls him close again. They are, I see, now the same height. Jordan takes her hand and won't let it go even when I embrace her and she whispers, 'He looks tired. Has he lost a little weight?'

Inside, in the bakery warmth of the kitchen, Jordan eats a plate of homemade cookies and drinks down a long glass of ice-cold milk. Mrs Lomax, knowing me as well as she knows Jordan, puts a bottle of Scotch in front of me and tells Jordan she'll help him get ready for bed. Jordan doesn't even bother to protest. He takes love where he can find it. I fetch the bags from the van and lock it up, carry them upstairs, and listen to Jordan and Mrs Lomax talking in the bathroom. Jordan's laugh reverberates round the tiles, Mrs Lomax sounds like a young woman on a date, her voice is high and light. She'll stay beside his bed until he sleeps. 'Just to settle him,' she always says. On our last visit I found them both asleep, their hands held tightly. She was sitting beside him in an austere wooden chair, sleeping upright.

I go back down into the kitchen, but the night is mild so I take the small measure of Scotch I've allowed myself and sit on the porch bench. There are no lights showing at Henry and Maude's. In the spare wash of the streetlights the house looks untended. I walk to the kerb then I cross the road and open the gate. The hinge is rusty and stiff, the path is scattered with litter. The storm door is broken and hangs loose. One of the gutters has come away and where the rain has flumed down, the boards are damp and the paint is

219

discoloured. I look back towards Mrs Lomax's house, trying to judge the feel: how does a house look when there are people in it? Beyond the lights, the shadows behind the thin curtains, does it give off a glow to show there is somebody living there? I hold my palm against the cold glass on the door and I know that Henry and Maude are gone.

At the back of the house, Henry's oil-drum barbecue is leaning against the fence. I lay it down like a body and the stagnant water collected inside it soaks into the grass. The white metal table has sheared from its legs. The top leans like a cartwheel against the wall. As I walk across the lawn, the house behind me blocks off the streetlights. Just the moon to light the way. Two steps further I trigger a security light next door. The garden is flooded with daylight and I see that Newton's swing has gone. Somebody has dug up the four concrete bases that anchored the legs. The holes are filled with compacted earth.

An old man's voice calls out to ask what I'm doing. I hear the false bravado. I call out that I'm staying with Mrs Lomax and that I came across to see Henry and Maude. He shouts that they've moved away and he's glad to see the back of them. Be even gladder when they sell the house and somebody starts looking after the property again. I tell him I'm sorry I disturbed him, he thaws and asks where I'm from but I don't want to get involved in the conversation so I go back out onto the road. The man shouts, 'So where are you from?' again. I set off towards the main street. A police car cruises past. It slows, I wave. The young man with the razor-cut hair looks me up and down, decides I pose no threat to the town and drives off, his podgy elbow leaning out of the window. The restaurant on the High Street is closed and dark as is the bar next door. A dog starts barking in the wire compound behind the fish restaurant. I walk along the porched wooden walkway past the chandler's, the deli, the general store from which the Keegans' name has been removed and the plastic generic of a national chain store put up in its place. The wooden boards have been stripped away and replaced by white plastic ones.

Just beyond the stores the raised walkway ends. I step down onto the unlit road and carry on towards the quay. A motorbike jets past like a comet of civilisation, then silence and darkness settle again. At the quay the black water slaps against the thick wooden pilings. I sit on the cold concrete, dangle my legs and, with a stone, chip at the barnacles that cling to the wood. A fishing line is caught among them like an empty string of pearls. I untangle the nylon and pull at it but it's knotted on something below me. The ferry is tied up for the night, the tyres along the edge bump gently on the quayside as the current hefts the hull up and down. A fishing boat chugs along the centre of the channel. A man is in the wheelhouse, standing and staring straight ahead of him. The boat slowly disappears into the mouth of the night. On the far side of the estuary a small yellow light glows like a gas-lantern.

The time passes slowly. The weather is mild but wet and Jordan is bored. He does not share my enthusiasm for long walks through the rain to the dunes to watch the heavy breakers corkscrew onto the beach. I have found a spot to stand which allows me to look down on the sea and watch it shift and shoulder and crowd itself until it spills with a sigh onto the shore. Jordan hates the taste of salt on his lips, the way it tangles his hair, the cold slap of spray on his face. Driftwood and its potential holds no fascination for him. He craves his pre-packaged thrills: TV, take-out food and the company of his friends. Mrs Lomax's attempts to entertain him have forced him to seek the sanctuary of his room. He hates Monopoly. He hates playing cards and no, he does not want her to teach him how to play chess. Mrs Lomax reverts to the kitchen and looks wounded when I get back from wherever I've been. I tell her not to take it personally. She says she is trying hard not to but Jordan was such a lovely child before, and do I wonder whether marrying a woman ten years younger than I am is the right thing for us?

The bar by the fish restaurant becomes my refuge and it is from there, two days before we are due to leave, that I call Carol. Four young hospital doctors have also set up base in there. Each year at this time, they hire a wooden shack on the mud ridge behind the dunes, raise the American flag, take off their watches, and drink the week away. They sleep when they feel the need, they eat when they're hungry and they walk for miles. Sometimes they swim naked by moonlight. One of them, an earnest, raggedy-haired blond anaesthetist, talks to me about the tyranny of time. What he says makes sense, but I'm never sure if they're taking the rise out of me. Whatever, they seem harmless and, like most medics, they seem sure of their place in the world: one step above priests, one step below God.

I take the phone to the end of the bar and lean over it like a miser counting his money. Carol answers her mobile and when I tell her who it is she asks me for the number and says she will call back. From her tone I can tell she's in a business meeting and not with Steve. I order another drink and watch the doctors try to build a castle of beer mats. All of them are smoking cigarettes. When they have finished their shared pack it gets torn ceremoniously apart. Everything they do has a ceremony attached. The phone rings and Carol tells me that this is a pleasant surprise and asks me what I want.

'I just wanted the chance to say goodbye,' I said.

'Why? Are you going somewhere?'

'I spoke to Steve's sister when you were away.'

'I know. She told me you'd called. She didn't tell Steve.'

'Good.'

'John. It's been three months. Why did you call?'

'I don't know. I just. I'm with Jordan on the coast and I was thinking about you and every time I think about you I remember how we parted and so I thought I'd call to apologise.'

'Steve and I separated.'

'You did?'

The beer mat castle collapsed. The cry from the bar drowned what Carol said next.

'I'm sorry,' I said, 'I didn't hear what you said.'

'He's already dating. I ran into him last week and he was with her. No shame. Not even a little remorse. What happened between you and me exonerates him from that.'

'Why did you decide to part?'

'He decided for us. She's a skinny girl, runny nose. I didn't think she'd be his type . . . So how is Jordan?'

'He's OK.'

'And how are you?'

'Me?'

'Yes.'

'OK.'

'Good. So have we finished, now? I mean, has this assuaged your guilt? Or was there some other reason you called?'

'No other reason.'

'Fine. Well it's been a real joy talking to you, John. I'm so glad we had this conversation and said all of the things we needed to say.'

'No. Look, I'm sorry.'

'You've already apologised. That's why you called.'

'I'm getting married, Carol. That's why I called.' And this is why. I needed to tell someone who would understand the significance.

'You called to tell me that?'

'Well, she hasn't actually . . .'

'Do you know something, John? Can I tell you something? One of the positive . . . no, the only positive thing to come out of my separation with Steve is that I have begun to enjoy sleeping on my own. I sleep soundly. Oh yes, and there is something else. I have learned to enjoy my own company. I find I am quite good company. I enjoy my point of view when I visit the cinema alone. I revel in remaining uncontradicted when I say that a concert stinks. It's not that I am short of men asking to take me out. What I am short of is a pension. But I intend to rectify this.'

'Should we meet?'

'Before or after you marry?'

'We're friends.'

'Married people don't have friends of the opposite sex. Anyway, we were never friends.'

'OK. Well, goodbye.'

'Goodbye.'

I waited. She waited. Then she said, 'See, we said it,' and put down the phone.

Out of the blue, when we got back, Angela called to tell us that she and Carl were taking a year out together. They were going to travel to India and take it from there. I said, 'Angela, we haven't spoken for six months, why do you assume I'd be in the least bit interested in what you and the moron are choosing to do with your lives?'

'Is it really six months?'

'Yes. More.'

'I'm coming round to apologise.'

'No need.'

'No. I Insist.'

I shouted to Jordan that Angela was coming round. He ran

out of his bedroom, grabbed his jacket from the coat-rack and sprinted towards the door calling something about going to the movies with Lindsay. I got there before him and barred the way.

'No,' I said. 'You don't get away that easily.'

'Dad. It's Angela!'

'So?'

'Angela . . . Come on.' He tried to push past. I held firm.

'Look. If I have to be polite to her then you do too. OK?'

'Unfair.'

'Life is unfair.'

'Yeah. And don't I know it.'

'Just say hello. Then you can go out.'

Jordan dropped his jacket on the floor and slouched back to his room. I stayed where I was, anticipating another surprise rush but his bedroom door slammed and the TV went on. I cleared up the room, not that it particularly needed it, but I wanted Angela to see that I'd got control of my life again. After I'd done that I changed my shirt and brushed my hair, then I cleaned my teeth.

When Angela arrived we tried to outdo each other with politeness. She expressed delight that I might be getting married. I apologised about calling Carl a moron, and told her I liked her hair short. I didn't mention that she looked like she'd had an extra chin grafted on. She said I was looking good too and had I lost some weight? When Jordan came in I offered Angela something to drink and she said that tea would be nice. Jordan volunteered to make it but I told him I'd do it while he talked to Angela because I knew he had to go out soon to the movies. He accepted the coded trade-off and sat beside Angela on the sofa while I went into the kitchen and turned on the kettle. As soon as I'd left the room the conversation seemed to dry up so, when I'd found the tea and the cups, in the new spirit of Glasnost I decided to go back in and break the ice. Just as I got to the door I realised that instead of an awkward silence, Jordan and Angela were actually talking very animatedly, but they were keeping their voices low so I couldn't hear. Through the crack in the door I saw Angela giving Jordan a hard time about something and him shamefacedly apologising. This was certainly not the mumbling adolescent boy I knew. This was a contrite, focused, adult version of my son. I remembered the letter Angela had sent him that he hadn't shown me and it came to me that there had been more and Jordan had revealed the contents of none of them.

The interrogation stopped. Angela's smile finished it. Jordan got up to go, Angela touched his face and pulled him down so she could kiss his cheek. He went to his room, reincarnated into a more familiar version of himself. I poured the tea and took the cups through. Angela was now up and standing by the window. She said, 'I was just thinking. Do you remember the first time we met?'

'Oh, yes.' I handed her her tea. 'You were acting as Susan's bodyguard. Hiding in the other room.'

'When you'd left I came back to see her because I knew you'd made an impression on her.'

'Yes?'

'And I knew that because of you she was going to die. I got quite hysterical. I had the most incredible sense of foreboding.' Angela, as usual, had lulled me into a false sense of security before springing the trap.

I looked over at Jordan's door. I didn't want him to hear this. The door was open an inch or so. It swung open further and Jordan came into the room. He was looking at Angela as if she had hypnotised him.

'Jordan, you can go now,' I said, but he didn't seem to hear me.

'But having Jordan here is like having Susan back again, isn't it John?'

'In a way.'

'Jordan,' I tried again, 'you can go.'

Jordan walked between us, took his coat and left. When the door closed behind him I said, 'Do you have any idea at all what he's been through?'

'Oh yes. Do you?'

'What?'

'Do you know what he's been through. What he went through before Susan died. Living with the two of you?'

'Don't even try it, Angela.'

'What can you mean?'

'There are no more paintings for you to remove. Leave me with the walls around us and the floor under our feet and leave me with what Jordan has become. Don't try and poison that.'

'I'm sorry.' She drew in a breath and expelled it. 'I'm sorry. I didn't come here to make your life any harder. I came to say goodbye.'

'Right.'

'Forgive me?'

'I expect so.'

Angela put down her cup and we embraced. Possibly our first embrace, ever, hard as that may be to believe. After that we managed fifteen minutes of relatively normal conversation: how was Carl, how long were they going for, what was I intending to do, what was Ottie like? But she couldn't leave it alone. She said, 'Jordan tells me they've had a good heart-to-heart.'

'Jordan and Ottie?'

'Yes.'

'Have they?'

'Apparently she told him that she'd tolerate him if he

didn't fuck with her or her mind. I think that's what she said
to him.'

'Ottie would not say that.'

'You don't know her, apparently.'

'Angela. I do know her. And you can't do this to me any
more. You can't hurt me. I didn't kill Susan. Ottie is a good
person. My life is stable. Jordan is no longer grilling
cockroaches. My alcohol consumption is under control.
There is nothing else you can do to hurt me. Nothing.'

'I didn't say you killed Susan. I said because of you, she
died.'

'Angela. Go to India. Don't come back.'

She put her hand on my knee and said, 'Do you know it
and won't admit it, or do you really not know it? She knows
it.'

'Goodbye, Angela.'

Central Park today is full of aged mothers with adult idiot
sons in overcoats buttoned up to the neck. Arm–in–arm, they
proudly perambulate, the women defying the world to think
anything less of them. I suspect it's the prelude to a march.
Maybe they've banded together in solidarity and they're
going to hold up the traffic on Fifth Avenue: The Simple
Sons Pride Parade. You rarely see men like these with their
fathers.

I have taken a roundabout route to the Boathouse Café
because I'm early. I've walked past the reservoir and cut
through Shakespeare Garden, and now I'm heading towards
Azalea Pond. The mild spell has broken and the temperature
has plummeted. The sky is heavy and white, harbouring an
immensity of elements. Any moment now it will unzip and
the lot will come pouring out like apples from a brown paper
bag. A group of birdwatchers has gathered by Belvedere
Castle. They are muffled against the November cold and a

woman, standing on a wooden box, is gesticulating in various directions provoking an orchestrated swing of binoculars.

'. . . American Robin, Black-Crowned Night Heron, Red-Breasted Nuthatch . . .' she intones, her voice catching and fading. As I pass a wave of warmth escapes from the midst of the group and the perfumed air briefly envelopes me. 11.55 now. 11.56. I cannot be early for Ottie, nor should I be late. Jordan and I discussed strategy over breakfast. We had not spoken about this day since I mentioned it a week before, but the first thing he said this morning was, 'What are you going to wear for Ottie?'

I hadn't thought, but Jordan had. He opened my wardrobe and took out my old black Comme des Garçons suit that Susan encouraged me to buy. Then he pulled out a white shirt and a striped tie. I was afraid he was going to want to come with me. Thankfully he didn't. He stayed with me as I dressed, nodded his approval, then went back to his room. Since Angela called he'd been different with me. More brusque and self-assured as if she'd told him to stand up for himself. Adolescence is going to be a bumpy ride for both of us.

11.57. Past Azalea Pond, between two clumps of trees, I catch sight of Willow Rock and the Eastern Point of the Lake. A small boy cycles past on a red tricycle, furiously pedalling, head down, scarf trailing. A father in jogging attire accelerates after him. He's pulling a small white dog along on a skateboard. The dog keeps jumping off, running alongside, then jumping on again. 11.58. Henry and Maude come into my mind. I wonder how Jordan would feel if we bought their house. I dismiss the thought. 11.59. With some of Angel's money I could set up a bursary for abstract artists and pay them not to paint.

Twelve o'clock and there's the Boathouse. Through the

windows of the restaurant a business group communes across a table. They're wearing dark suits with white shirt cuffs. One of the men is leaning back, talking into a mobile phone. A waitress attends them, patiently taking the ribbing she's receiving. Another attractive waitress is looking out of the window, focusing somewhere in the middle-distance. I cross her field of vision and she blushes and smiles. I smile back and take a seat outside, at the café end of the building. Here the birdwatchers and the regular users congregate eschewing the New York swank of the restaurant for the homely comforts of the café's sandwiches and soup. It's a place that, like most outdoor cafés, comes into its own in the winter and the hardier regulars vie for who'll sit outside the latest in the year. Still no sign of Ottie.

12.01. I brush away the crumbs from the table and decide to wait for her to arrive before I order. The thought of her warms me. The birdwatchers pass in a noisy chattering group, heading for the Model Boat lake. They don't stop, for which I am thankful. 12.02. I try to recall our last conversation. All I can remember is that she said, 'You'll have your answer, I promise.' And only now do I hear the edge in her voice and wonder if that was, indeed, her answer.

12.03. 'Is this seat taken?' An old lady has decided to join me. Several other tables are empty but she's looking for company.

'I'm afraid it is,' I say, smiling, 'I'm waiting for somebody.'

'I'm sorry,' she says in a warm voice tainted with loneliness. She goes to the far edge of the island of tables and sits down, placing her large black bag in front of her. She undoes the clasps and takes out a clear plastic envelope of new money. She slides out a single note and waits for somebody to come and attend to her.

12.04. I remember now telling Ottie that the man I am is

not the man I was and I wonder if I should have pressed my case a little harder. It's too late now and, anyway, it was a lie. We never change. We can't. All we can do is access our core in different ways. That's what I was trying to do with Cynthia, but I failed.

12.05. Perhaps my watch is fast. A young, balding, troubled man passes carrying a book-store bag. I call out to ask him the time, he keeps on walking, half turns and says, 'Five after twelve.'

'Thanks,' I call.

'No problem.' He faces front and heads quickly away.

12.06. A twin-bladed military helicopter passes overhead travelling north. When the noise of it has abated the sounds of sirens rush to fill the silence. I need the silence to be filled because I am still trying to drown Angela's bitter insinuations. It begins to rain. The old lady goes inside to find a table in the warm.

12.07. In the distance, coming towards the café from Tupelo Meadow, I see a woman. She's wearing a long black coat and a red scarf. She looks like Ottie; roughly the same height and build, but from this distance it's too early to tell.

12.08. My thoughts turn to Newton and all that remains of him: the dip in the lawn scuffed by his toes as he slowed the swing. When they played together Jordan used to push Newton higher and higher until he called, 'Don't make it go too high!' This was the cue for Jordan to push him harder still. There was a complicity between the two boys not so different from that which exists between many mothers and their sons. It's a complicity that men search for in other women they meet and love and it's a profound moment when they learn they can't have it. It must be harder still when circumstances conspire to make a son believe he's lost his mother.

12.09. I think about my grandfather and the engine shed

and the dark mornings and a hand holding mine all the way
to the bus stop. I wish I'd known my father. I'm sure he'd
have given me the strength that I just can't seem to find.

12.10. I can see the woman clearly now and it's not Ottie.
Maybe I'll order a coffee anyway and give her ten minutes
more. I have no other plans for the rest of the day.